The Twinkling Tutu

Gwyneth Rees is half Welsh and half English and grew up in Scotland. She went to Glasgow University and qualified as a doctor in 1990. She is a child and adolescent psychiatrist but has now stopped practising so that she can write full-time. She is the author of the bestselling Fairies series (*Fairy Dust, Fairy Treasure, Fairy Dreams, Fairy Gold, Fairy Rescue, Fairy Secrets*), *Cosmo and the Magic Sneeze, Cosmo and the Witch Escape, Cosmo and the Secret Spell* and *Mermaid Magic*, as well as several books for older readers. She lives near London with her husband, Robert, their daughters, Eliza and Lottie and their two cats, Hattie and Magnus.

Visit www.gwynethrees.com

Gwyneth Rees

The Twinkling Tutu

Illustrated by Jessie Eckel

MACMILLAN CHILDREN'S BOOKS

For Lottie,

with love

First published 2011 by Macmillan Children's Books
a division of Macmillan Publishers Limited
20 New Wharf Road, London N1 9RR
Basingstoke and Oxford
Associated companies throughout the world
www.panmacmillan.com

ISBN 978-0-330-46116-0

1 3 5 7 9 8 6 4 2

A CIP catalogue record for this book is available from
the British Library.

Printed and bound in the UK by CPI Mackays, Chatham ME5 8TD

1

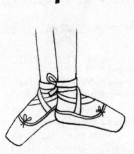

'Dad, *why* can't I come with you today?'
Ava asked as she watched him ring the
doorbell of her Aunt Marietta's dress shop.

'I've already told you, Ava,' her father
replied a little impatiently. 'I'm going to be
too busy to look after you properly once I
get there.'

'I don't need *that* much looking after,' said
Ava huffily. 'I'm nine, Dad. I'm not a *baby*.'

Ava could hardly believe how much
her life had changed in the last two weeks.
When she had first arrived at Dad's house
at the start of the summer holidays, she had

been an ordinary girl coming to spend the summer with her divorced father while her mother went away on a once-in-a-lifetime sailing trip. Then, within days, her life had been turned completely upside down after she had discovered that her dad had a younger sister – Marietta – who she had never met before, and who owned a clothes shop just round the corner.

Only it had turned out to be no ordinary clothes shop . . .

From Marietta, Ava had learned the secret her father had been keeping from her for all this time – that he came from a long line of people who were able to travel via magic portals to other times and places. The portals existed in the form of magic mirrors – of which Marietta had many in her shop – and you could travel through them if you were

2

wearing the right magic clothes.

The portals not only transported you to *real* times and places in history, Ava had

discovered. A week
ago she had put on
a beautiful magic
princess dress and
made her first
journey through
a magic portal to
Cinderella-land –
just in time to
attend Cinderella's
marriage to Prince
Charming.

As her dad and aunt had explained,
the mirrors acted as magic gateways *only*
for those few families – like Ava's – who
possessed the travelling 'gift'.

3

It had been a lot to take in for Ava – who hadn't even really *believed* in magic until then.

The shop door was flung open suddenly and Marietta appeared, beaming at both of them. Her long red hair was loose and rather wild-looking, as if she hadn't got round to brushing it yet that morning, and she was wearing one of her brightest green medieval-style dresses. 'Come in, come in,' she invited them at once. 'Sorry the door was locked but I haven't had time to open up properly yet.'

Ava's father, who was so used to Marietta's eccentric clothes that he rarely seemed to even register them, frowned as he glanced down at his watch. 'We *are* a bit early but I want to get going as soon as possible.'

 4

'That's all right, Otto. And don't worry.
I've got everything you need laid out
ready for you.' She smiled warmly at Ava.
'You and I are going to have a lovely day
together, Ava. I can't leave the shop, because
I'm expecting an important visitor, but don't
worry – I won't let you get bored!'

'What visitor?' Dad asked.

'Oh, nobody you know, Otto,' Marietta
replied swiftly.

As she spoke she led them through the
small front section of the shop, which
had several racks of dowdy second-hand
clothes on display, and which Ava knew
was only a cover for what the shop really
contained. Through an archway in the
back wall, screened off by a multicoloured
beaded curtain, was a totally different room.
Marietta called it her fairy-tale room as it
contained dozens of beautiful gowns fit for
a fairy-tale princess to wear. The walls were
painted with colourful scenes from different
fairy tales, and in the centre of the room a
gold spiral staircase led both upwards – to
Marietta's special fairy-tale wedding section –
and downwards to a room Ava had yet to

 6

see. In one corner there was a changing cubicle with a gold sparkly curtain pulled across the front, where Ava had changed into her fairy-tale outfits on her previous visits.

Today Ava's father was planning to travel back to Victorian times – and Ava desperately wanted to go with him.

'Marietta, don't *you* think Dad should take me with him?' Ava said to her aunt. 'I mean, what's the point in me finding out about the magic portals if I'm never allowed to use them?'

'The point, Ava, is that you have many years ahead of you in which to use the portals,' her father interrupted crisply. 'And you've already travelled back and forth through one of them several times, despite knowing about their existence for barely a fortnight. I don't think that's the same as never being allowed to use them, do you?'

Ava had to admit that what he said was true. But that didn't stop her feeling frustrated that her father seemed reluctant to let her use her newly discovered gift any further. Marietta thought she should be allowed more freedom to try out the magic too, but unfortunately Marietta's views didn't hold much weight with Dad. (Marietta was ten years younger than him and from what Ava could gather he tended to be overprotective of *her* as well.)

'I bet if Mum knew about all this, *she'd* say I could go with you today,' she said.

Her dad let out a dismissive snort. 'Come off it, Ava! If your mother knew anything at all about any of this, she'd be back from her sailing trip like a shot and taking you straight home with her!'

Ava knew that he was right, of course. Although her mother could be fairly lenient when it came to letting her do certain things, this would more than likely totally freak her out. Ava's mother didn't possess the travelling 'gift' herself and she knew nothing at all about it – or about the existence of Marietta and her shop.

Ava's parents had split up a year after she was born, and Ava's father had managed to keep his secret from his wife during the brief time they had been together. Ava hadn't seen much of her dad since then – until this summer, when Mum had asked him to take care of Ava while she was away for six weeks. Ava realized that her mum was counting on this time to give Ava the chance she had always wanted to get to know her dad better.

9

If only Mum knew how *much* better, Ava thought now.

'Besides,' her dad went on, 'today I need to be able to concentrate on the job I have to do – not on looking after you, Ava. And I'm afraid Victorian London isn't like Cinderella-land. It's no place for you to be roaming about unsupervised.'

'*I* roamed about in worse places than that on my own when I was younger than Ava,' Marietta pointed out.

'Yes, well, *our* mother and father weren't exactly the most responsible of parents, were they?' Dad answered her swiftly.

Marietta sighed. 'They were certainly much more carefree than you are, Otto,' she agreed. 'But oh – we did have a lot of fun when we were children, didn't we?' She laughed as she added, 'Remember that

 10

time they left us on that pirate ship for a day?'

'I *do* remember,' he answered crossly. 'The pirates threatened to make us walk the plank, and you could hardly swim at the time. We were lucky nothing terrible happened to us!'

Marietta laughed. 'I suppose it did get a bit hairy at the end, right enough.' She put one arm round Ava's shoulders as she guided her for the first time through a door in the back wall of the fairy-tale room. 'Come and see my Victorian room, Ava,' she said.

Ava found herself in a narrow, dimly lit corridor that had doors opening off it on either side. All were closed except for a door at the far end, and it was to this one that Marietta led Ava and her father.

'What do you think?' Marietta asked as she stepped inside.

'Wow!' Ava exclaimed as she followed her.

For the room didn't just contain racks of Victorian clothes. It had been decorated to resemble a small Victorian living room. There was an open fireplace, and the mantelpiece above it was full of old-fashioned china and glass ornaments, with a large rectangular mirror hanging from the picture rail above. A red velvet sofa sat in front of the fireplace, and the walls, decorated in a bold gold-and-red patterned wallpaper, were heavily covered with Victorian paintings and more ornate mirrors of different shapes and sizes.

'I've put the clothes you'll need through there in the dressing room, Otto,' Marietta

 12

told him, pointing to a door that led off
from the room they were in. She winked
at Ava as she added, 'Wait till you see the
transformation that's about to take place,
Ava. Your dad is about to change from his
usual scruffy self into the most fashionable of
Victorian gentlemen!'

'Are the clothes here *magic* like the ones in
the fairy-tale room?' Ava asked as her father
disappeared into the dressing room and shut
the door behind him.

'Of course,' Marietta replied. 'Can you
guess which one is the magic mirror that
transports you back to Victorian times?'

Ava glanced around the room, inspecting
each mirror in turn. Eventually she pointed
to a large, heavy-looking oval wall mirror
with an ornate gold frame that was situated
on the back wall. 'I don't know why, but

 14

I've just got a *feeling* it's that one,' she said
tentatively.

Marietta beamed
at her. 'See – it's
obvious you are
perfectly ready to
travel just like I
was at your age.
Do you hear that,
Otto?' she shouted at
him through the closed
dressing-room door. 'Ava's instincts
are already telling her the right mirror to
choose. That means she's more than ready
to travel through the mirrors by herself!'

'*I'll* decide when she's ready, thanks,
Marietta,' Ava's dad grunted back.

Unable to take her eyes off the mirror,
Ava begged, 'If Dad won't let me go

through on my own, then can't *you* come
with me today, Marietta? Just for a little
while . . .'

Marietta looked sympathetic as she
replied, 'I told you, Ava. I have to wait here
for my visitor and he lives quite far away so
I've no idea when he'll get here.'

When the dressing-room door opened
several minutes later and her father stepped
out, Ava could hardly believe at first that it
was her father.

'*Wow*, Dad!' was all she could manage to
blurt out.

Standing in front of her was a Victorian
gentleman in a smart three-piece suit and
top hat. His long flared black jacket came
down to his knees and was unbuttoned to
reveal a grey waistcoat with front pockets
that held a gold watch and chain. He also

wore a wide, elaborate grey necktie, and
the top hat was made
of dark felt and had a
wide ribbon encircling
the base.

'Oh, Dad, *please*
can you take me
with you?' Ava
pleaded again,
longing to dress
up in a Victorian
outfit herself.

'Ava, I've
already told
you – I need
to be able to
concentrate
on my work
today,' he replied

a little impatiently. As Ava scowled at him he continued, 'You remember that Victorian nanny I met before? Well, she's arranged for me to interview a ballerina who happens to live next door to her.'

'A ballerina?' Ava queried in surprise. She knew her dad – who wrote historical books – did all his research by actually visiting the appropriate period in history, but as far as she knew he was currently writing a book on a totally different subject. 'I thought you said you were writing about the lives of Victorian *children*,' she said.

'That's right. You see, in 1861 – which is the year it is on the other side of our magic mirror at the moment – children who performed on the stage had to work

 18

extremely long hours with very little regard for their safety. This ex-ballerina, Madame Varty, apparently set up a *reformed* sort of ballet school, where young girls could learn in much better conditions than they had done previously. But she isn't mentioned in any history books on the subject – which is why I'd like to interview her for mine.' As he spoke he pulled out what

looked like two very ancient theatre
tickets from the inside pocket of his jacket.
'You may as well look after these for me,
Marietta,' he said.

'Are you sure you won't need them this
time?' Marietta asked. 'You are writing
about the ballet after all!' She turned to
Ava and explained: 'The theatre tickets
that come with this suit are very special,
Ava. Every time you take them through
the magic mirror, whatever date it is on
the other side automatically appears on
them. And since the theatre in question is
very close to where our portal opens up in
Victorian London, it means you can easily
go and see whatever's on. They've got a
ballet running at the moment.'

'Not really my cup of tea,' Dad said,
pulling a face.

 20

'I love going to the ballet!' Ava told them enthusiastically. 'All those gorgeous outfits, and the ballerinas are SO graceful . . . I just wish I could dance like that! I had ballet lessons when I was little, but the teacher told Mum I had no coordination and that I was the most un*bendy* child she'd ever taught! Mum was really cross with her and stopped taking me after that!'

Marietta and Dad both laughed, and Marietta placed the theatre tickets behind one of the candlesticks on the mantelpiece for safe keeping.

'I'll see you both later,' Ava's dad said as he went over to stand in front of the magic mirror, staring into it intently as he waited for the bright glow that signalled the start of the magic reaction. Ava knew that,

21

when it came, the brightness would quickly
fill the whole room and be so unbearable
that she would be forced to close her
eyes – and that when she opened them
again her dad would be gone.

'Come on, Ava,' Marietta said, putting
a gentle hand on her shoulder. 'I've made
some new girls' princess dresses with
matching hats that I'd like you to try on
for size for me. And I could do with some
help sorting through an order of crowns
that came in yesterday. You don't mind, do
you?'

'Of course not!' Ava exclaimed
enthusiastically, her attention immediately
diverted from her dad.

'Good! Let's get started straight away!'

And as Ava followed Marietta out of
the room she glanced back only briefly at

 22

her dad, who was concentrating so hard
now on his reflection in the mirror that he
barely seemed aware she was still there in
any case.

2

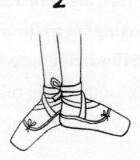

'So who's this important visitor you're
expecting today?' Ava asked Marietta a little
later that morning as she stood on a chair
helping to arrange the five latest sparkling
gold crowns on the shelf with all the others.
She had already tried on the stunning new
princess dresses and found that they all fitted
her perfectly.

Instead of replying, Marietta pulled out a tarnished-looking crown from the back of the shelf and showed it to Ava. 'Just look at this old thing – one of the rubies is coming unstuck from it again. Maybe it's time I binned it.'

'You *can't* put a ruby crown in the dustbin!' Ava protested in horror.

Marietta laughed. 'The rubies don't become *real* until they're on the other side of the magic mirror, remember.'

'I know, but even so . . .'

'Well, don't worry. What I mean is that I'll send it off to a special recycling bin. All the new crowns that came today are made from recycled old ones. The magic in them is never lost – it just gets transferred from the old ones to the new. Luckily there are some very specialized recycling businesses run by certain families who have the travelling gift.'

'What about the magic dresses?' Ava asked curiously. 'Do *they* get recycled as well?'

'Oh, yes – as soon as they get too old to be worn any more,' Marietta told her. 'The magic thread in them gets extracted and I get it sent back to me in the form of brand-new reels.'

'Everything about your magic shop is quite complicated, isn't it? But so exciting as well!'

Marietta smiled as she replied, 'Don't worry, Ava. I'm sure you'll soon get the hang of how it all works.'

Suddenly Ava remembered her original question. 'Marietta, you said that you were expecting an important visitor today . . .'

'Oh, yes . . .' Marietta looked slightly cagey as she told Ava, 'It's an old friend of my father who contacted me recently. He couldn't say exactly when he was coming, so I promised I'd wait in for him.'

'A friend of your father? Really?' Ava was immediately interested.

Something else she had only just found out that summer was that her grandparents on her father's side *hadn't* actually died before she was born as she had always been told. Instead it turned out they had left the real world twelve years earlier to go and live for good in one of the fantasy lands they had discovered. Since such a thing was completely forbidden, they had destroyed the portal they travelled through so nobody could follow them – and nobody had seen or heard from them since.

'That's right. I can't say I ever remember hearing my father talk of him – but apparently the two of them knew each other when they were very young.'

'Why is he coming to see you?' Ava asked.

'He sounded very secretive on the phone,' Marietta replied. 'He said that he had some information about our parents that might interest us, but that he wanted to give it in person.'

Ava felt her excitement mounting as she thought about what this could mean. 'Do you think this man might actually know where your parents *are*? Do you think he might have a message from them?'

But Marietta was frowning now and looking flushed. 'Ava, I just don't know,' she said a little sharply. 'I haven't even *told* your dad about it yet because he'll only get himself all worked up, and there may not be

 28

anything worth getting worked up *about*. Do you understand?'

Marietta was obviously much touchier on the subject of her parents than Ava had previously realized. Not wanting to upset her further, Ava quickly nodded and suggested they try on some more clothes while they waited for Marietta's visitor to arrive.

'OK then,' Marietta agreed, sounding relieved at the prospect of the distraction. 'What is it you want to try on?'

'Something Victorian, please,' Ava said at once, nearly bouncing up and down with delight at the thought.

So after they had finished tidying all the crowns and tiaras they headed back to the little room at the end of the corridor.

This time Marietta led Ava straight

through to the dressing room. It was a bigger room than Ava had anticipated and she saw at once that *this* was where most of the Victorian outfits were kept. There was a small area of free space in one corner where a chair (currently strewn with Dad's discarded clothes) had been placed, and there were some hooks on the wall above it for people to hang things. But the rest of the room was crammed full with rack upon rack of Victorian clothes.

'Are these dresses *all* from the Victorian period?' Ava asked in surprise, because the ladies' gowns hanging on the nearest rail seemed to be so varied in style. There were heavy silk dresses with massive crinoline skirts, brightly coloured satin gowns with huge bustles extending out from the back, and tighter, more figure-hugging gowns with

lots of ruffles and pleated frills. In addition, a
wide shelf on one wall was piled high with
a huge variety of ladies' headwear – straw
hats with pretty ribbon streamers, heavily
decorated bonnets with high brims that tied
in big bows under the chin, plainer bonnets
with veils attached, and small linen indoor
caps decorated with lace and ribbons.

'Oh, yes,' Marietta replied. 'Queen
Victoria was on the throne for a very long

time, remember, so fashions changed a lot throughout that period. In 1861 – which was around the middle of Queen Victoria's reign – the crinoline dress was in fashion. You wore a wire hoop cage underneath your skirt to hold it out. Even young girls like you wore them. You can try one on if you like. I've got a whole rack of children's clothes here somewhere.'

'Oh, yes please!' Ava exclaimed enthusiastically as she watched her aunt squeeze behind the front rail of elegant gowns to reach the other racks behind.

'Hey, look what I've just found!' Marietta suddenly gasped in delight as she held up a child-sized Victorian ballet costume to show her. The Victorian tutu wasn't anything like the short, stiff, sticking-straight-out-from-the-waist sort of ballet tutus that Ava was

 32

familiar with. It was longer, much fuller
and more free-flowing, made of several
layers of very fine white netting that gave
it a delicate, floaty look. It was attached
to a white-satin bodice that had a scooped
neckline edged with lace, and short off-the-
shoulder sleeves. The bodice was decorated
at the front with delicate pink
and gold beadwork and the
mesh of the skirt also had
beads embroidered on to
it – shimmering pinky-pearl
ones and gold-flecked glass
ones – which gave the
tutu a very eye-catching,
twinkling appearance.

'Oh, *please* can I
try *that* on?' Ava
begged.

Marietta smiled. 'Of course. Look –
there's a pretty cape here too and a little silk
bag with ballet shoes inside. Oh – and you
can wear this with it as well.' She lifted up a
pretty hair wreath decorated with large silk
white daisies and passed it to Ava along with
the little shoe-bag. Ava quickly
undid the bag and took
out a pair of white satin-
covered pointe shoes.
They looked in perfect
condition, as if they had
never been worn.

As Marietta squeezed out from between
the clothes rails, holding the ballet dress and
cape, she glanced at Dad's clothes strewn
over the chair and muttered, 'I wonder
how your dad's getting on. I just hope he
doesn't say anything to offend this ballerina

he's gone to interview – he never *has* liked ballet.'

'He didn't offend anyone when he came to Cinderella-land with me,' Ava pointed out. 'In fact he seemed much more polite to everyone *there* than he is to people in the real world!'

Marietta laughed, agreeing that there was probably nothing to worry about.

She carefully hung up the tutu and the cape on the free hooks and stood back with Ava to inspect them. The cape had three layers and was made from very fine cream material decorated with hand-embroidered flowers and trimmed with fancy scalloped edging. 'The cape will help keep you warm,' Marietta said, turning round to point out a small wooden trunk pushed against one wall. 'And if you look in there you should find

some stockings that will fit you too. Now –'
she glanced at her watch – 'as you know, I
have to stay in the shop today, but I don't
see any reason why *you* shouldn't go on a
little journey through the mirror by yourself
if you want to, Ava.'

For a few moments Ava wondered if
she'd heard her correctly. 'Really? But Dad
said—'

'I know what Otto said, and of course it's
totally up to you . . .' Marietta interrupted
at once. 'But if you want my advice . . .
well . . . let's just say that if I was you, I
wouldn't let your dad stop *me* from doing
what I was born to do. The travelling gift
is a part of you, Ava – and if you miss out
on making the most of it now, you'll never
get this time back again.' She sounded
extremely passionate as she added, 'Your

 36

dad thinks you should use your gift sparingly until you're an adult, but I disagree. Believe me, Ava, some of the most exciting travel adventures you'll ever have are now, while you're still a child, not later when you're grown up!'

'But I don't understand,' Ava said, feeling confused. 'Do you mean you think it's OK for me to disobey Dad?'

'Not usually, no,' her aunt replied. 'But he is SO protective about travelling, he always has been . . . and on the other side of the Victorian portal there's another shop and the owner of it is a travelling person too. If you decide to go there then I know he'll look after you.' And before Ava could say anything else, Marietta had given her an encouraging smile and swiftly left the room.

Ava's confusion rapidly started to change

into excitement as she unbuttoned her cardigan at the same time as kicking off her sandals. Her aunt had almost made her feel as if it was OK to disobey her dad and go though the magic mirror on her own. *Almost . . .*

One thing she was sure of was that she couldn't wait to see what she looked like dressed as a Victorian ballet dancer – and when she finally inspected herself in the full-length mirror on the back of the dressing-room door, she could hardly believe the transformation. The floral wreath was a little too big for her head and the pointe shoes a little tight, but apart from that the whole outfit – including the cape – fitted her perfectly. Her feet looked very dainty in the shoes fastened on with their pink criss-crossing ribbons.

But the most amazing
thing was the tutu itself,
which seemed to be
twinkling with an almost
visible magical energy
now that she was
actually wearing it.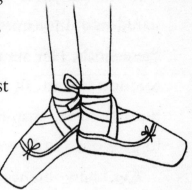
The beads in the skirt
were sparkling like miniature jewels and Ava
could hardly take her eyes off them.

She was certain that if she stood in front
of the magic mirror dressed like this it
wouldn't take long for the portal to open
up. But should she actually go ahead and use
it?

She went through to the little Victorian
sitting room, walking slowly over to stand
in front of the magic mirror. No ordinary
person would guess that the mirror was

special in any way. Yet Ava knew that if she stared into it for even a few seconds wearing these clothes she would cause the magic reaction to start. In fact, even as she stood there thinking that, the mirror was starting to give out a little warning glow.

Ava knew she had to turn away at once if she wanted to make the magic reaction stop, but she found herself thinking about how badly she wanted to see Victorian London. What should she do? Marietta thought she should ignore her father's instructions and go. In fact Marietta had made it sound as if *not* going was something Ava might regret for the rest of her life. But what about her loyalty to her dad? And what would he say if he found out?

Ava's reflection in the mirror was glowing more strongly now, and she still hadn't quite made up her mind. But her feet seemed to have decided for her, because she found herself staying put exactly where she was in the mirror's glow. Her head felt swimmy and all she could hear was the sound of her pulse racing inside her ears. Seconds later she couldn't see her reflection any more because the light was so dazzling. The magic had already taken hold . . .

As she closed her eyes against the glare

she knew that when she opened them again she would be in Victorian London. And that's when she stopped feeling uncertain and started to feel determined – determined that after she got there she was going to prove she was perfectly capable of taking care of herself, despite her dad's misgivings!

Ava opened her eyes to find that she was inside what seemed to be a smart Victorian furniture shop, facing her reflection in a large oval-shaped wall-mounted mirror very similar to the one in Marietta's shop.

Her head was still spinning and she stood where she was, waiting for the dizzy feeling to pass.

As she caught her breath she saw that the mirror had a little card tucked into the bottom inside edge of the frame, which said NOT FOR SALE in curly old-fashioned writing.

43

Turning round she immediately saw the reason for the card. The shop sold several other grand-looking mirrors, in amongst other items of expensive-looking furniture. Clearly the shop's owner only had the one portal mirror and wanted to make sure that it didn't accidentally get sold. Strangely though, there was no sign of the shopkeeper, or any customers.

Ava began to make her way towards the door, taking care not to bump into any of the pieces of ornate furniture as she squeezed past. She edged round an impressive display of shiny mahogany tables of various shapes and sizes, all of them with beautifully carved legs, then sucked in her tummy to pass between two high-backed velvet-upholstered armchairs.

Dad must have been here too this

 44

morning, Ava thought – but where had he gone after that?

As soon as she stepped outside she knew the answer.

She was in a wide Victorian street on a lovely sunny summer's day – a street that had upmarket shops on one side and large detached houses on the other. And in the house immediately facing her two young girls in ballet costumes could be seen peering out from a large ground-floor bay window to admire two fine-looking ladies in crinolines and pretty bonnets who had stopped to talk to each other in front of the gate.

This is amazing, Ava thought, feeling like she was walking around in the middle of a dream.

There was no sign of Ava's father, but

Ava was sure that the house opposite
must belong to the ballerina he had come
to interview. She waited for a horse and
carriage to pass, before crossing the
cobbled street to the other side. One of the
ladies glanced at her briefly as she passed
through the small iron front gate and up
the gravel drive that led to the porch of the
house.

Since this was clearly the perfect house
to visit if you were dressed as a Victorian
ballet dancer, Ava reached up and rang the
doorbell without hesitation. She wasn't sure
exactly what she would say when the door
was opened, but she knew she would think
of something. Marietta had told her that
the magic power in the clothes meant that
nobody on the other side of the portals ever
asked too many questions about who you

were or where you came from. And that
had certainly been true in Cinderella-land,
where no one had ever questioned Ava's
disguise as a royal princess.

The front door was quickly opened by a
thin, sour-faced young girl in a
Victorian maid's uniform, who
took one look at what Ava was
wearing and admitted her into
the house without question.

Ava found herself in a
large, very grand hallway,
which had a wide curved
staircase ascending from it.

'All the other girls are
waiting in the drawing room,
miss,' the maid said, showing
Ava into a room off the hall.
'Madame Varty will send for

you when she's ready.'

'Excuse me,' Ava said quickly, deciding it was better to know for sure if she was in any danger of bumping into her father or not. 'I think a . . . a writer gentleman was coming here this morning to interview Madame Varty. Do you know if he's still here?'

'There *was* a gentleman called to interview her this morning,' the maid replied. 'He said the nanny from the house next door had told him about Madame's school. Madame sent him away but said she would see him if he came back later this afternoon. Now . . . I really must be getting on with my work, miss.'

Since her father clearly wasn't here any more, and since he hadn't returned to Marietta's shop, Ava could only assume that he had gone off to explore some more of

Victorian London on his own. Which was really unfair of him, she thought crossly, since he knew how badly she wanted to visit Victorian times and he could quite easily have come back to fetch her.

Ava turned to inspect her surroundings and saw that she was in a typically cluttered Victorian drawing room along with a little group of other girls in ballet dresses – much simpler than Ava's – who were all standing staring at her.

'Why are you so late?' one of them asked. 'Not that it matters! We've been waiting here for almost an hour already. Why, our mothers will be coming back to collect us soon!'

'Did you really wear your pointe shoes out on the *street*?' another girl said, sounding horrified. 'My mama would have a fit if I did that!'

 50

'Aren't you going to wear your hair *up* for the audition?' asked a third girl, reaching up to touch her own hair pinned into a neat bun. 'It doesn't look very tidy like that, you know.'

'Oh, let her be,' said yet another girl, giving Ava a little smile. She was looking at Ava's ballet dress admiringly. 'I do *so* love your tutu. I've never seen one like it before, with all those pretty beads sewn on to it! Your cape is very pretty too. What's your name? *I'm* called Victoria – after the Queen, of course.'

'I'm Ava,' Ava said, smiling as she removed the cape and placed it over the arm of the nearest sofa.

Before Victoria could say anything else, the girl who had first spoken said snootily, 'Well, Ava, just because you have a much

fancier tutu than the rest of us, it doesn't
mean you'll definitely get a place here. My
mother says only the most *talented* girls will
be accepted for Madame Varty's school.'

'Yes, and my ballet teacher says I have
more talent than any other girl she has
ever taught!' boasted the girl who had
commented on Ava's hair.

'Really? That's exactly what *mine* said as
well,' Victoria put in grinning. 'I think they
all say that because they know how it pleases
our mothers!'

At that moment, a different young maid
entered the room and gave them all a
friendly smile. 'Madame Varty is sorry to
have kept you waiting and she says that she
will see you now,' she told them.

'What, *all* of us?!' exclaimed the girl
nearest the door in surprise.

'Yes, miss. I've to show you all up directly.'

Ava quickly decided that she may as well stick with the other girls for now. It wasn't as though she could wander around the streets on her own for very long dressed as she was without drawing attention to herself and, besides, she was curious to meet the ballet teacher Dad seemed so impressed by.

The maid led them back out into the hall and up the grand staircase to the next floor. From there she led them along a corridor and into a very large room at the back of the house. As Ava stepped inside she saw that this room, in contrast to the drawing room downstairs, was very sparsely furnished. It had a wooden floor with no rugs and was almost completely empty apart from a massive open fireplace and a large, very

beautiful mahogany piano at one end, where
a grey-haired woman in a dark crinoline
dress sat on a stool watching them.

Standing in the centre of the floor, dressed
in a very glamorous turquoise crinoline
gown, was a fine-featured blonde-haired

woman who Ava assumed
must be Madame Varty. She
was much younger than Ava
had expected. Her shiny
hair was done up in an
elegant roll on top of her
head and she had high
cheekbones and bright,
inquisitive blue eyes. She
was looking at all the
girls with undisguised
curiosity as they each
lined up in front of

her and gave her a respectful little curtsy.
Ava, who was the last in line, also curtsied
before following the others as they were
waved across to stand at a long practice bar
attached to the far wall. There were several
large mirrors placed around the room and as
Ava caught sight of herself in one of them
she realized that her hair *did* look terribly
messy compared to the neat buns of the
others.

Madame Varty moved across the room
towards the girls – who numbered eight in
total – and it was only then that it became
apparent that she was leaning on a thin,
silver-handled wooden cane and that she
walked a little stiffly.

'Good morning, young ladies,' she began
in a crystal-clear voice that held just the
trace of a foreign – possibly French – accent.

'I am Amelia Varty, but you may call me
Madame.'

'Good morning, *Madame*!' they all
chorused back obediently.

'As you probably know, I have recently
returned from Europe to set up a new ballet
school here in London – one that will take
in mainly paying pupils like yourselves, but
only pupils who show real talent. I shall also
be offering places to one or two girls who
shall board here with me and be taught for
nothing, purely because I believe they have
exceptional talent. All my girls will be treated
equally, whether they are paying pupils or
not.' She paused. 'I intend my ballet school
to be a shining example to others. It will
not only be exemplary in its high standard
of teaching but in the fact that the *health and
safety* of my dancers will be prioritized at

 56

all times. And when my pupils are ready to perform in public, I shall not be hiring them out to any theatres with poor safety records or unacceptable working conditions.' She paused again before adding in a quieter voice, 'I myself know only too well the cost of performing in such places.'

Ava couldn't help wondering what had happened to her, but was afraid that it might sound very rude to ask. In any case Ava guessed that was the sort of thing her dad would be finding out when he interviewed her for his book.

'Now . . . I know that all of you have high hopes of becoming pupils at my school. But if I feel you would *not* benefit from a place here I shall tell you so at once. This may be hard for you to hear – and even harder for some of your mothers – but nevertheless I believe it is important to be honest from the start. I shall speak to all of your mothers personally when they call back to collect you.' She paused, looking in turn at each girl as if to assess the affect her words had had on her.

As she looked at Ava she frowned and called out to the lady at the piano, 'Some

hairgrips please, Anna.' The older woman immediately rose and went over to the mantelpiece to pick up a small wooden box, which she brought over to the ballet mistress. Ava was bright red in the face as Madame Varty plucked off her floral headband and proceeded to pin up Ava's hair with a deftness that was impressive.

She clapped her hands together to silence
the other girls, who had all started to giggle,
before sending Ava back to stand in line.
'Quiet now . . . Take a place at the bar, all
of you, and let us do some simple exercises
to warm up. Then I shall ask each of you
to perform the audition piece you have
prepared for me.'

Ava felt her heart start to beat faster.
She had attended only a handful of ballet
lessons back when she was five – and she
could hardly remember any of the steps she
had learned then. And as for performing an
audition piece . . .

She suddenly realized she ought to leave
before she made a total fool of herself – but
how?

Her stomach had already started to churn
alarmingly which made it pretty easy to

pretend to be ill. Clutching her middle, she mumbled an apology and ran across the room to the door.

She heard Madame Varty calling out after her, but she didn't look back as she headed for the staircase, hurrying down it as fast as she could. Unfortunately her exit from the house was blocked by one of the maids who was standing in the doorway greeting a rather grand-looking lady in a large hat. Ava darted into the drawing room instead, but found that it contained the two ladies she had seen outside, still talking animatedly to each other as they took off their bonnets and silk shawls. These must be two of the girls' mothers, arriving to wait for them, Ava thought, briefly wishing her own mother wasn't so far away as she escaped back into the hall.

She tried the next door along, which
opened into a large airy room with windows
that looked out on to the back garden, but
that room was also occupied. The young
sour-faced maid was there, along with a
short wiry-looking middle-aged man dressed
in dark grey baggy clothes, brightened by
a gaudy red scarf tied around his neck.
Neither of them seemed to have heard
Ava come in as they continued to stand
with their backs to her in front of the large
marble fireplace – out of which, to Ava's
amazement, a pair of small blackened feet
could be seen protruding!

Ava noticed then that the floor of the
room was covered in sheets of brown paper,
the curtains had been taken down from
the windows, the dining table and other
furniture had been covered with large dust

sheets, and
that all the
pictures on
the walls had
cloths draped
over them.

'You find
that little imp
or I'll light
a fire under
both of yer,' the man was snarling at the
pair of disappearing feet. For a moment Ava
remained puzzled, then she realized that the
man must be a chimney sweep and that the
feet must belong to his climbing boy. 'He's
small enough, that littl'un I sent up first,
so he can't 'ave got 'iself stuck,' the master
sweep was saying to the maid.

'The other one looks like he might do

though,' the maid replied. 'He's a big lad to
be sendin' up a flue, ain't he?'

'They're brothers – I'm doin' them a
kindness to let 'em work together,' the
sweep grunted defensively. 'The littl'un's
handy for gettin' into tight places an' the
bigger one keeps 'im from gettin' too scared
and freezin' stuck on me. Though what's
happened to 'im today, I don't know!'

Ava suddenly felt worried as she
remembered something her father had
told her recently about Victorian chimney
sweeps – that child sweeps sometimes got
stuck in narrow chimneys and suffocated.
He had once seen it happen with his own
eyes – and it was something that still upset
him when he talked of it.

The master sweep didn't seem the least
bit worried however. 'Where's she from

then, this grand lady of yours?' he asked the
maid as he scratched his nose with a sooty
finger.

'She's just moved back to England from
abroad,' the maid told him, clearly enjoying
the chance to gossip. 'All I know is that she
used to be a ballerina – quite a famous one
in foreign parts, so they say – but something
happened that meant she couldn't dance no
more. She was widowed very young, so Mrs
Potter our housekeeper says, and she doesn't
have no other family. She was left this house
by her great-aunt and she's going to turn it
into a ballet school.'

'A ballet school, eh?' The sweep had
produced a long brush and he was pushing
the stick end of it up the chimney after his
climbing boy. 'Get a move on, you little
beggar!' he shouted up at him gruffly. 'We

'aven't got all day!' He turned back to the maid with a sly look on his face. 'I don't s'pose you've some straw or a bit of wood for me to light in the grate?'

'Whatever for, when it's the middle of summer?' the maid exclaimed in surprise.

'To get those lazy little beggars to move a bit faster, that's what for,' answered the sweep, giving her a devilish grin.

This was too much for Ava, who could keep quiet no longer. 'You *can't* light a fire under them!' she shouted in horror. 'I won't let you!'

The sweep and the maid both jumped.

'Ee, it's just one of Madame's girls,' the maid said, recovering quickly as she recognized Ava. 'What are *you* doing in here, miss? Why aren't you upstairs with the others?'

At that moment another servant, who Ava hadn't seen before, entered the room. Judging by the woman's age and her attire, she looked like she might be the housekeeper.

'There you are!' she exclaimed when she saw Ava. 'The mistress sent me to find you – as if I haven't got anything better to do this morning! Come on! You're to come back upstairs with me at once.'

'But there are two boys up that chimney, and this man's going to light a fire under them!' Ava burst out. 'You've got to stop him!'

To Ava's dismay, the housekeeper just laughed dismissively, saying she didn't care *what* the sweep did, as long as it resulted in her chimneys getting cleaned. 'And it's no business of yours either, miss,' she told Ava

sharply, attempting to take hold of her by
the elbow and escort her from the room.

'Don't you touch me!' Ava snapped,
pulling her arm away roughly.

Just then the door opened again and
Madame Varty limped into the room,
causing the master sweep to bow his
head politely and the young maid to do a
respectful bob.

'Would someone kindly tell me what is
going on here?' the ballet teacher demanded.

'It's this naughty girl you sent me to look
for, Madame,' the housekeeper declared
hotly, pointing at Ava. 'She won't let the
sweeps get on with their work!'

'That's not true! I only want to stop them
lighting a fire under the boys who've gone
up that chimney!' Ava burst out, close to
tears now.

Madame Varty frowned questioningly at the master sweep. 'Surely the child is mistaken?'

The sweep just shrugged.

Madame Varty turned to address her housekeeper. 'Surely *you* would not let that happen, Mrs Potter?'

At that the housekeeper quickly changed her tune. 'Not me, Madame, no. It was the sweep himself and the servant girl there who were about to do it.'

'Well, I absolutely *forbid* such a thing to take place in my house,' stated Madame Varty crossly, glaring at the sweep and the young maid with knitted brows. 'Is that clear?'

The servant girl looked close to tears, but the sweep merely replied evenly, 'Whatever you say, m'lady. Not that they'd have come to any real harm. A little scorchin' of the feet never did any permanent hurt an' it's a kindness really, as it encourages 'em faster up the flue an' they breathes in less soot that way.'

Madame Varty looked sceptical, but instead of responding she turned her attention back to Ava. 'You, young lady, are to come back upstairs with me at once. There is only one cure for stage fright in my opinion – and that is to force oneself to dance in spite of it.'

'But I haven't *got* stage fright,' Ava protested. 'I just don't want to audition any more, that's all.'

'Nevertheless you *must*,' the ballet mistress insisted vehemently. 'To have insufficient talent is one thing – but to allow *fear* to hold you back is quite another.'

'Oh, but I *do* have insufficient talent,' Ava attempted to reassure her. 'Honestly, I have absolutely no talent *at all*!'

But Madame Varty clearly wasn't about to accept Ava's word for it, and Ava saw that

71

the only way she was going to convince her was to actually demonstrate that fact. And it was only then that another thought suddenly occurred to her. Her ballet dress was magical, wasn't it? So was it possible that here, on this side of the portal, she *would* be able to dance after all?

4

As Ava stood in the middle of the room
at the start of her audition she felt trembly
and completely clueless about what to do
next. If the magic in the ballet tutu *did* give
the ability to dance to whoever wore it, it
clearly wasn't taking hold immediately.

Then, just as she was giving up on the
prospect of any magical help and resigning
herself to being totally humiliated in front
of everybody, there came a sudden loud
banging noise over by the chimney.

As everyone in the room turned to look
the banging got louder, clearly coming from

inside the chimney. A cloud of filthy soot suddenly billowed out into the room, closely followed by a little black bundle of rags that cried out in pain as it landed with a thud on the tiled hearth.

Chaos immediately broke out, with some of the girls screaming and all of them clambering to get as far away as possible from the little bundle, which Ava now saw was a small child covered from head to toe in black soot. The child was trembling, its eyes fixed and staring like a rabbit caught in headlamps.

As Madame Varty clapped her hands together to try and restore order, the child remained transfixed, its eyes wide with wonder at the sight of all the little ballerinas in their pure white clothes. Then the master sweep, who must have heard all the commotion from downstairs, came charging into the room to grab the child – which produced even more screams from the hysterical ballet girls.

Seeing that this was her chance to escape, Ava followed behind the master sweep as he dangled the little climbing boy by the scruff of his tunic and bumped him roughly down the stairs. Mrs Potter the housekeeper was standing below them in the hallway, holding the front door open as she screeched, 'Lift him up off my carpet, you wretched oaf!

You're putting soot everywhere!'

The master sweep grinned, clearly enjoying upsetting the housekeeper as he turned to the little climbing boy and said, 'Look at this, Fred. We're bein' shown out the *front* door today, we are!'

'You're not taking him through my nice clean house to get to the back!' the housekeeper yelled. 'And don't think we'll be having *you* sweep our flues again, not if I have any say in it!'

The sweep mumbled something rude at her under his breath as he pushed the boy down the front steps, with Ava following close behind. Mrs Potter either didn't notice or didn't care that Ava was leaving too as she slammed the door shut behind them.

As the sweep gave the boy a kick to get him to his feet, he declared, 'I'll give you a good beatin' when we get back, that I shall. An' now I've got to go an' find that wretched brother of yours. If *he* gets stuck up there an' never comes down again, it'll be you that's to blame, boy – just you think on that.' He gave the child another kick in the direction of the path that ran up the side of the house where some cats were fighting over a pile of fish heads and other scraps that had been left out for them. 'You can wait there by that pile o' stinkin' scraps. At least then I won't forget where I've left you.' He didn't seem to even register that Ava was there as he strode off towards the back of the house.

Ava waited until she was sure the sweep was gone before going over to the little boy, who she could hear crying softly. He looked two or three years younger than her and

77

much smaller and thinner, dressed only in a ragged tunic and trousers that left his filthy arms and legs bare. He had taken off his cloth cap to scratch at his hair, which was totally caked in soot. In fact, every part of him was black with soot, apart from his eyes, which were sore and red as he rubbed away tears.

'Oh, you poor thing!' Ava exclaimed, nearly in tears herself at the sight of him.

The boy looked frightened and shuffled away from her. His elbows and knees were bleeding and his tunic was badly torn. He quickly replaced his cap as if that would afford him some sort of

comfort, then took it off again as he realized he must show respect in the presence of a lady.

'Is there anything I can do for you?' Ava asked, squatting down beside him. 'Your name's Fred, isn't it? Mine's Ava. Would you like me to fetch you a drink or something?' Ava was sure that whoever owned the furniture shop across the road would provide her with a cup of water.

At first she thought the boy wasn't going to speak, but then he suddenly whispered, 'Me brother, miss . . . is 'e safe? Did you see 'im?'

'I saw his feet disappearing up the chimney when they sent him up after you,' Ava replied.

'They didn't light a fire under 'im, did they? The master is always playin' that trick.'

'No – the lady who owns the house wouldn't let him light a fire,' Ava said. 'Oh, but your master's a horrible man! Isn't there some other job you and your brother could do? Surely you've some family who can help you?'

The little boy looked at her as if he was starting to think she might be a figment of his imagination. 'I don't know of no other job, miss. And me family is the ones who sold us to the sweep.'

'Your mother and father *sold* you?!' Ava exclaimed in horror.

The boy shook his head. 'Our mother's dead an' our father couldn't cope no more so 'e took us to live with our aunt and uncle. He said he'd come back an' fetch us, but he never did. It was our uncle who sold us, after he got fed up waiting for our pa.

 80

He didn't want no children to bring up, he said – especially ones that weren't his own.'

'But that's terrible!'

'They live in the next street from here,' the boy added. 'The master said 'e went an' asked them this mornin' if we could do their chimneys too, but they wouldn't hear of it. Tom thinks they'd feel too guilty, seein' us like this.'

'Tom's your brother, is he?'

The little sweep nodded. 'He looks after me. I just hope I haven't got 'im in no trouble. I got lost in those crooked chimney passages, see. I didn't mean to scare all you young ladies when I fell down the wrong flue.' The boy paused, a strange look on his face. 'For a minute I thought I'd died an' gone to heaven, seeing you all there. I even thought I saw our mother. That were a sweet moment! Then the master came for me and I knew I was just imaginin' it.'

'I don't understand,' Ava said, puzzled. 'Do you mean you thought we were angels or something?'

'Oh no, miss – I could see you was ballerinas. Like my mother was 'fore she died . . . Ever so beautiful she was . . . Sometimes she'd let us watch her from the side of the stage while she rehearsed, and we'd see the other dancers too. It was like being back with her again, seeing all of you jus' now . . .' A tear rolled down the boy's face, which he quickly wiped away.

'Your mother was a ballet dancer?' Ava asked gently.

The boy nodded. 'An' I was going to be one too, but Tom says I never will now.'

 82

'Did you like dancing too then?' Ava asked in surprise.

The boy nodded. 'My mother said she thought I'd be just as good as her one day. But Tom says I've to forget about all that now, or else the two of us won't be able to stay together.'

'I suppose it's mainly girls who become ballet dancers anyway, isn't it?' Ava said slowly.

The child gave her a strange look. 'There are boy dancers too, miss, but in any case I *is* a girl. Me real name's Florrie. Our uncle let Tom cut off my hair and pretend I was a boy so Tom and me could stay together. Girls ain't meant to go up chimneys, see, tho' I knows I ain't the only one what does.'

Ava just stared at the little sweep, completely amazed.

'Miss, can I have that drink o' water now?' Florrie asked shyly.

Ava quickly came to her senses. 'Of course. Why don't you come with me to fetch it?' She stood up and held out her hand.

'Oh, you mustn't touch me, miss. I'll cover you in soot!' the child exclaimed, sounding horrified.

'It doesn't matter. I can wash it off,' Ava said, wondering when the little sweep herself had last been washed, she was *so* filthy.

'I'd best stay here in case the master comes back,' Florrie said quickly. 'Don't worry about fetchin' me any water if it's a trouble for you, miss.'

'It's no trouble, but . . . Florrie, how old are you?' Ava suddenly asked.

'Near enough eight, miss.'

 84

'And how long have you been working as a chimney sweep?'

'It's been almost two years now, miss.'

'And have you practised any dancing in all that time?'

'Not much, miss. Sometimes I do a little if I'm not too tired. But mostly I'm too sore to dance.'

Ava frowned thoughtfully, hardly daring to hope that her idea might work. 'And you say your mother thought that you were a *very* good dancer?'

'That's what she said, and she was a ballerina herself. But Tom says as how mothers always think that, whether it's true or not.' Florrie shrugged. 'It's no matter now, in any case.'

Ava squatted down beside Florrie again. 'Listen, Florrie . . . what if you had the chance to go to a ballet school? One where you would be taken care of *and* learn to be a dancer like your mother.'

Florrie was silent now, looking as if she thought Ava might be a little mad.

'Listen,' Ava said urgently. 'The lady who lives in this house is setting up a new ballet school. She's holding auditions for pupils today – mostly paying, but she's also going to take on one or two girls for free. They'll be allowed to live here in this house and attend her school for nothing – but only if she thinks they're exceptionally gifted. It sounds like *you* might be the sort of girl she's looking for. Do you think you could audition for her?'

The little sweep was staring at her in disbelief as if she couldn't believe what she was hearing. 'But how can I go to an

 86

audition dressed like this, miss?'

'You won't *be* dressed like that!' Ava was getting excited now. 'You can borrow what *I'm* wearing. I know this ballet tutu will be a bit big for you, but I'm sure we can adjust it somehow. You'll need a wash, of course, so we'll have to find somewhere to do that. But if you come with me, I think I know where we can get some help.'

Florrie was clearly in two minds about whether to trust Ava or not. And she was obviously worried about going off without her brother. But the expression on Ava's face was so genuine and Florrie badly *wanted* to trust her. It was just that nobody apart from her brother had shown her any kindness in such a long time that it was difficult. However, Florrie could still remember a very different life from the

87

one she led now, where there had been no
shortage of people who cared about her.
Perhaps it was the memory of that other life
that gave her the courage to stand up and let
Ava take her hand . . .

Together the two girls walked across
the road to the furniture shop, the sight
of them hand in hand causing quite a stir
among some lady shoppers on the pavement
opposite. The shop had a side entrance and
Ava instructed Florrie to go round to the
back of the building to wait for her. Then
she took a deep breath and went inside the
shop, hoping that the owner would be there
this time and willing to help.

'Can I assist you?' asked a crusty voice
from behind a desk in the corner, and Ava
saw an elderly man peering at her over the
top of his gold-rimmed spectacles.

 88

Ava decided there was only one thing to do. Since there were no other customers she said shyly, 'My name's Ava. I'm . . . I'm a travelling person . . . My aunt Marietta said you would help me . . .' She trailed off, watching his face closely.

He was silent for a few moments. 'I don't travel much myself these days,' he eventually

grunted. 'But I'm always happy to help those who do. What is it that you need?'

'Somewhere to get changed, please,' Ava said quickly. 'And some soap and water and a place to wash.'

The old man frowned. 'You don't look particularly dirty to me.'

'It's someone *else* I need the soap and water for,' Ava explained.

'I see.' The old man looked puzzled, but he also looked like he had heard stranger requests before from his travelling customers. 'You'd better come out back then. I can't promise much *hot* water, you understand, but I'll see what I can do.'

5

In the little kitchen area at the back of his
shop the old man heated up a large pan of
water on the iron range and poured it into
a tin tub for Florrie to use as a bath. He also
found them a bar of soap and a towel. Then
he left them to it.

Looking as if she thought she
must be dreaming Florrie
stripped off her
filthy rags and
climbed into
the tub a little
nervously. It

91

turned out that she couldn't remember the last time she'd had a bath, and that much chimney soot wasn't easy to get off. On seeing the task that lay ahead of them, the old man had given them quite a generous amount of hot water, even putting another pan on the stove to heat up so they could fill the tub a second time if necessary.

It clearly *was* necessary, for by the time Florrie – with some help from Ava – had thoroughly scrubbed her completely sooty body and black-as-tar hair, the first tub of water was as black as she had been herself. Once Florrie had stepped out of the tub and wrapped herself up in the towel, the old man came back into the kitchen. He took the tin bath and emptied it into the back alleyway before filling it again with clean water. The little half-washed sweep cowered

shyly behind Ava all the while.

This time Ava concentrated on scrubbing the remaining coal tar out of Florrie's hair, feeling thankful that at least it was cropped short so that there wasn't much of it to do. 'There's not enough of it to go into a bun, but we can use my hairpins to pull it back off your face,' Ava said. 'The white stockings will completely cover your legs, so the only parts that will be showing are your face and neck and arms. Let's try and get those as clean as we can, shall we?' As she applied what was left of the soap as vigorously as she dared, the little sweep whimpered a little. 'I'm sorry. Am I being too rough?' Ava asked gently. 'I'll try not to start your poor elbows bleeding again, but we've really got to get more dirt off or you won't look right.'

'Are you sure 'tis all right for me to wear
your lovely things, miss?' Florrie asked her
for the umpteenth time.

And for the umpteenth time Ava replied,
'Yes – otherwise I wouldn't have suggested
it! And please just call me *Ava*!'

When they were finished Ava couldn't
help smiling at the change in the sweep's
appearance. Her hair was a whole shade
lighter and her face was almost free of
soot entirely. Her skin still had a greyish
appearance in places and the scabs and cuts
on her limbs were pink and even more
obvious now than they had been before her
bath. But all in all Florrie looked a lot less
like a chimney sweep and a lot more like
a normal little girl. In fact she was rather
pretty!

'Right,' said Ava, starting to undress

 94

herself. 'Gosh – I've got these ballet clothes quite sooty, haven't I?' She should have changed out of the ballet clothes before she helped Florrie with her bath, she realized. Still, at least now the tutu looked a bit less perfect than when she had worn it herself – as if it might well belong to a poorer girl who couldn't afford ballet school fees. 'If these shoes are too big for you we can stuff some crumpled paper in the toes,' Ava added as she undid the ribbons.

'What are *you* going to wear, miss?' Florrie asked, drying herself quickly before accepting the ballet dress from Ava.

'I guess I'll just have to wear your tunic and trousers,' Ava replied, sitting down to take off the ballet shoes and remove her white stockings. 'I reckon I should be able to fit into them since they seem quite big for you.'

'They're big because they're Tom's old ones,' Florrie told her. 'But, miss, they are little more than rags and *so* dirty—'

'It doesn't matter,' Ava interrupted swiftly with a smile. 'And as I want to blend in out there as a chimney sweep I'd better make the rest of me dirty too.' She glanced across at the small kitchen fireplace. 'I guess I'd better use some soot to blacken my skin a bit,' she said. 'I can rub some into my hair as well.'

'You can put my cap on your head and tuck your hair up under it if you like, miss,' Florrie suggested.

So while Florrie changed into Ava's ballet outfit, Ava set about turning herself into a convincing chimney sweep, rubbing soot into her arms, legs and face and putting on Florrie's discarded clothes, which felt as rough as sandpaper against her skin.

Both girls let out exclamations of surprise as they turned to face each other.

'You look so different!' Ava burst out. 'No one would ever believe you were the same person!'

Florrie spun on the spot delightedly as the tutu twirled and twinkled about her. 'Nor would they *you*, miss!' she added when she stopped.

'Come on,' said Ava excitedly, leading the

way out through the open back door. 'You
must go straight to Madame Varty's and ring
the bell as confidently as you can. If you tell
the maid who opens it that you're there for
the audition today, I'm sure she'll let you in.'

'Do you really think so, miss? I mean, I
don't look as fine as all those other girls, and
it's not like they're expecting me. And what
if the maid turns me away? I'm not sure I
am brave enough to say anything if she
does . . .' Suddenly Florrie's bottom lip
started to tremble.

Ava frowned, wishing she could introduce
Florrie to Madame Varty herself, but of
course now that they had swapped places
that was impossible.

Then she had an idea. 'I know! I'll write
you a letter to take with you – a letter
of introduction! They can hardly refuse

that – and then *you* don't even have to
speak, Florrie!'

'A letter . . . ?' Florrie sounded uncertain.

'Yes. It can say that you're an orphan –
that your mother was a ballet dancer and
that you are also very talented, but that
you have no money to pay the tuition fees
for her school. We just need to find some
paper and a pen . . . maybe *you* should
write the letter rather than me because
my handwriting isn't going to look very
Victorian . . .' Ava trailed off as she saw the
expression on Florrie's face.

'*I* can't read or write, miss!' Florrie was
looking at Ava incredulously.

'Oh, of course not,' Ava said hurriedly.
'Maybe we could ask the old man in the
shop to do it. Yes . . . you wait here for me
and I'll go and speak to him.'

Ava emerged
from the back of the
shop ten minutes
later holding an
envelope addressed to

Madame Varty in curly Victorian script.

'Here,' she said, giving the envelope to
Florrie. 'All you have to do now is get the
maid who answers the door to take this
straight to Madame Varty.'

'But what shall I dance at the audition?'
Florrie asked uncertainly.

Ava frowned. 'Isn't there something your
mother taught you?'

'There *was* a piece my mother learned me.
I've been trying to remember it, but I can
only think of the beginning.'

'Maybe the rest will come back to you
when you start dancing,' Ava said, trying

to sound confident, even though she was beginning to feel a bit nervous herself. What if Florrie *couldn't* remember and wasn't deemed good enough after all for a place in Madame Varty's school? Ava would have got Florrie's hopes up for nothing – and probably got her into terrible trouble with the cruel sweep master as well.

Florrie however was starting to look *more* confident, lifting up her small chin in a determined way as she replied, 'You know, I'm sure I can feel my mother looking down on me from heaven. If I think of *her* as I dance, she will help me remember.'

'Good.' Ava gave her an encouraging smile as they set off. 'I'll just come across the road with you and wait at the gate to check they let you in.'

Florrie smiled back at her gratefully.

'There's one more thing, miss. If you meet my brother, you mustn't tell 'im where I am. He made me promise not to dance no more, see.'

'But surely if you actually got a place at Madame Varty's school . . . ?'

'Tom wouldn't let me audition if 'e knew, miss. I know 'e wouldn't!'

'Well, don't worry. I won't tell him where you are,' Ava reassured her, but at the same time she couldn't help thinking that it was a bit strange that Florrie's brother was so set against his sister following in their ballerina mother's footsteps. She understood his desire to keep them together, but if it came to a choice for his sister between the dangers and hardships of being a sweep and the magic of being a ballerina, surely he would understand?

★

Ava looked on from the bottom of the drive as the friendlier of the two young maids opened the front door and accepted the letter of introduction from Florrie. The maid immediately invited Florrie inside, presumably to wait in the hall while she took the letter upstairs to her mistress.

Ava was intending to wait for just long enough to ensure Florrie wasn't refused a chance to audition. After that she planned to walk around the streets by herself for a little while, just to see how it felt to be a barefooted chimney sweep in Victorian times. But as she stood there Ava was suddenly hailed by another barefooted figure, hurrying towards her from up the road, carrying a tankard of something. It was another child chimney sweep, a year or so

older than Florrie, who Ava guessed must be Tom, the little girl's brother.

'Hello,' Ava called out, attempting to give him a reassuring smile. He was slightly taller than Ava, a lot less fragile-looking than Florrie, but still covered from head to toe in black soot, with blood running down from one knee.

He looked puzzled as he inspected Ava, as if she didn't seem like a normal climbing boy, but he couldn't quite put his finger on why. He obviously didn't notice that she was wearing his sister's clothes as he said, 'I'm lookin' for a little lad. Like me, only smaller and thinner. I hope he ain't run off. Our master's gonna thrash the both of us somethin' terrible if 'e has.'

'You mean Florrie. Don't worry. She's fine,' Ava told him quickly.

'You *know* Florrie?' The boy looked at her suspiciously. 'Wait a minute. Yer a girl too, ain't yer?'

Ava nodded. 'Florrie and I . . . just met and had a . . . a little talk.'

The boy frowned. 'What sort o' talk were that then?'

'Oh . . . well . . . she was just telling me how your uncle sold you to that horrible chimney sweep,' Ava replied, deciding it

was probably safest not to say too much
about their conversation.

But even that mention of his family
seemed to infuriate Tom, who stamped
his foot on the ground in frustration. He
started speaking very rapidly. 'Don't tell
me she's gone back to find our uncle's
house? I was afraid she'd try that when
she knew we was workin' in the next street.
An' she can't miss the house on account
o' that big ugly lion statue at the gate.
She keeps thinkin' our father will go back
there to find us one day, only I keep tellin'
her 'e must be dead 'iself or he'd have
come back and fetched us in the first place
like he promised.' He shook his head
angrily. 'Now she's goin' to get us in a
whole lot of trouble. What am I to do?
The master's sent me out to buy him some

ale and 'e told me to check if Florrie was still waitin' where he left her and to bring her back too. *Now* what am I gonna tell him?'

As they stood there, neither of them noticed that the master sweep had appeared from the side pathway to the house and was now standing scowling in their direction. Suddenly he yelled at the top of his voice. 'You get back 'ere this minute, you lazy little beggars – or I'll thrash the both of you!'

Tom looked panicky. 'He thinks *you're* Florrie,' he said, 'or Fred, as he calls her, tho' I'm sure he must've cottoned on by this time that she's a girl.'

'Why don't I come with you for now – just to buy Florrie some more time?' Ava offered, thinking that, above all, she didn't want any sort of commotion to ruin Florrie's audition.

Tom looked grateful. 'What do they call you anyhow? Live round 'ere, do you?'

Ava told him her name, thinking very fast before adding quickly, 'I'm here with my father.'

'Oh yeah. Do you work for 'im then? Is 'e a sweep too?'

Ava didn't answer as she followed Tom along the path that led round the side of the house. The master sweep had already gone on ahead of them, clearly assuming they would follow. 'Tom, won't your master *know* I'm not Florrie as soon as we get close enough for him to have a proper look?' she asked him, anxious about it suddenly.

'There's a good chance he won't bother getting any closer to you than this. He's been

 108

ranting on about how he can't stand the sight
o' Florrie at the minute on account o' 'er
coming down the wrong chimney. If we're
lucky we might get you up the flue without
him gettin' a proper look at yer at all.'

'Oh, but I couldn't actually *climb* a
chimney!' Ava gasped.

Tom gave her a strange look. 'It's a funny
kind o' chimney sweep who can't climb a
chimney!' he declared.

'I know, but . . . but you see, I've never
been up one before!' Ava said, flushing.

Tom looked perplexed. 'Are you kiddin'
me? I thought you jus' said your father's a
sweep an' you work for 'im?'

'Yes, but . . . but . . .' Ava began, trying
to think how to talk her way out of this.
'He hasn't actually sent me up a chimney
yet, you see . . . Or shown me how to do it.

Is it . . . is it *ever so* difficult?"

Tom looked incredulous. 'He's left it a
bit late to start you off, hasn't he? You'll be
too big to be any use to 'im soon. An' how
comes you're so sooty already if you haven't
even been up a flue?'

Ava shrugged, not knowing what else she
could say.

Tom let out a loud sigh. 'Well, don't
worry because it's pretty easy once you get
the knack. You jus' push yer way up by
pressin' your knees and elbows against the
sides of the flue, see. When yer shoulders
and yer elbows are fixed firm, you shuffle
yer legs up. Then, when yer legs are fixed,
you shuffle your shoulders up. As you're
shuffling, you sweep most of the soot away
and you only sometimes need to use a
scraper for the hard stuff. But listen . . . you

 110

don't want your first time up a flue to be with *my* master underneath you. You best forget it.'

But before Ava had the chance to forget it, she found herself at the rear of the house being grabbed, not by the master sweep, but by Mrs Potter. 'Gotcha, you little wretch!' the bad-tempered woman grunted.

Ava screamed and tried to struggle free, but it was no use.

That's when they saw that the master sweep was sitting some distance away on an old tree stump at the bottom of the garden, munching a pie. He waved Tom over and immediately grabbed the tankard of ale from the boy. 'Mrs Potter's found just the chimney for you to climb, young Fred,' he shouted across to Ava. 'A nice straight one where you can't get yourself lost! Be careful you don't get stuck though, for it's a narrow one when you get near the top, so she tells me!' He chuckled. 'And be glad you're good and skinny, for it wouldn't help you to have a big fat bellyful of dinner inside you, like your poor master here.' He belched loudly.

'Your poor master's just tramped his muddy boots all through my beautiful clean house, so I've told him he can stay out here while *I* take you inside,' grunted the housekeeper sourly.

'Let *me* go up that flue for you, missus,' Tom offered at once. 'I'm a much quicker climber than me brother is.'

But Mrs Potter just shook her head, tightening her grip on Ava's arm as she told Tom, 'Don't you worry. I'm sure a few pins stuck in his feet will help him go faster – and I've a sewing box full o' them!'

'Let me go!' Ava shouted, starting to struggle.

'You're bigger an' heavier than I thought you were, lad,' Mrs Potter complained as she dragged Ava into the house. 'I fear you're going to have a terrible job squeezing up this narrow flue. Still, it's like I always say, the more you climbing boys have to wriggle, the more soot you scrape off in the process!'

6

The housekeeper dragged Ava into a small sitting room at the back of the house, where she half pulled, half pushed her over to the fireplace. There she forced Ava's head and shoulders up into the chimney opening where Ava cried out in shock as her face was scraped against the inside wall. The movement dislodged a lump of soot, which stung her eyes and filled her nose so that she started to cough uncontrollably. And at that point, Ava really panicked, kicking out her feet with all her might and catching the housekeeper in the belly. As Mrs Potter

yelped and loosened her grip, Ava shoved
both hands as hard as she could against the
sooty walls, pushing herself downwards out
of the flue. And before the cruel woman
could grab hold of her again, Ava had
dodged past her and escaped from the room.

Ava bolted down the corridor in the
direction of the open back door where Tom
was still standing. Wide-eyed with surprise
at the sight of her, he stepped back to let
her past, then grinned suddenly as he moved
back into the path of the housekeeper,
causing the woman to waste precious
seconds before she could continue her
pursuit.

The sweep master, who was still enjoying
his lunch break in the sun at the bottom
of the garden, stood up and let out a shout
when he saw what was happening. Then

he put down the rest of his lunch and gave chase as well. Fortunately Ava had a good head start as she streaked across the road, darting behind a passing horse and cart as she headed for the furniture shop.

The old man got up from his desk when she entered, but there was no time to stop and speak to him as she rushed by, squeezing between the high-backed chairs and skirting round the collection of grand tables to get to the magic mirror. Once there, she stood in front of it, panting, as she stared at her reflection in the glass.

But this time, instead of immediately starting to glow, the mirror didn't do anything. She glanced quickly about her to check she had the right one, but this was the only mirror with a little card saying NOT FOR SALE on it. She stared at her

 116

reflection again, willing
the magic to start up,
but for some reason
the mirror didn't seem
to be reacting to her
presence at all.

And that's when
she suddenly realized what the problem
was. Since she had exchanged outfits with
Florrie, she was no longer wearing any of
the magic clothes from Marietta's shop!

As the shop door was flung open by a
very angry Mrs Potter, Ava did the only
thing she could think of. She dropped out of
sight behind the nearest table.

'Where is he?' Mrs Potter demanded of
the old man, who had turned slowly to greet
her.

'Where is *who*?' the old man asked quietly.

'The sweep's boy of course! I just saw him run in here, the little wretch! When I get hold of him I'll give him such a whipping! I'll flay the skin off him, that I will, afore I hand him back to his master.'

The shopkeeper pointed to the door that led out the back to the kitchen. 'I believe he went that way,' he said coolly.

At that moment, the sweep master burst into the shop too, and the old man pointed him in the same direction. 'I don't know if you'll catch him. There's an alleyway out back. He may be gone by now.'

The second they had both disappeared, the shopkeeper beckoned for Ava to come out of her hiding place. 'You must return at once to wherever it was you came from,' he whispered to her urgently.

'I *can't* return,' Ava said, starting to cry

a little with frustration. 'I need my magic clothes but I've given them away. Oh . . .' Suddenly she remembered something.

'My cape!' she gasped. 'I left it in Madame Varty's drawing room. If I wore that, would it be enough to transport me home again, do you think?'

'I should think any part of your costume ought to suffice,' the old man replied. 'Make haste though. You must go and fetch it while those two are looking elsewhere.'

So Ava hurried back across the road and up the driveway of the house, where she paused for a moment, knowing she couldn't call at the front door dressed as she was. She quickly made her way round to the back, where she found Tom sitting in the garden, looking gloomy. He stood up, however, when he saw Ava.

'So they *didn't* catch you,' he said, coming across the grass to join her. 'That's a good thing for you, but it means they must still be thinkin' you're Florrie. She's goin' to get a terrible beatin' when *she* turns up again.' He frowned, clearly still worried about the whereabouts of his sister. 'If she doesn't come back soon I'm goin' to have to go to our uncle's house and look for her there,' he grumbled.

'I'm sorry, Tom,' Ava said sympathetically, 'but I haven't got much time to talk to you. I need to go back inside the house and find something I left there.'

Tom shook his head at her as if he couldn't believe her foolishness. 'Well, if they catch you, don't expect *me* at yer funeral.'

Nervously she stepped in through the

120

back door, hoping that the corridor Mrs Potter had dragged her along would take her to the front of the house. Luckily it did, for it was a servants' passageway that led all the way to the entrance hall where it came out via a small door behind the staircase. She stood for a moment in the empty hall, hearing piano music coming from the upper floor. She briefly wondered how Florrie was getting on at her audition, but of course there was no time to wait around and find out.

She soon identified the drawing-room door and as she pushed it open she heard ladies' voices talking politely inside, and the sound of china teacups chinking against saucers. It appeared that several more of the ballet girls' mothers had now arrived to wait for their daughters.

None of them spotted Ava creeping silently into the room and hiding herself behind the nearest high-backed armchair.

Ava could see her cream cape, draped over the arm of the sofa where she had left it – but how was she to fetch it without anybody seeing her?

She quickly got down on her hands and knees and started to crawl behind the furniture as quietly as she could towards the sofa and her cape. As she crept along, she listened with interest to the ladies' conversation, for they were talking about Madame Varty. Several of them had seen her performing in the past, and one lady began to talk in a hushed tone about how unfair it was that Madame Varty would never be able to dance again. It seemed from what the lady was saying that Madame Varty

had initially suffered a relatively minor injury
to her knee, from which she would have
recovered had she been properly looked
after by her ballerina employers. Instead she
had received no treatment at all and had
been made to keep working long hours on
stage despite her injury. As a consequence
further damage had been done to the knee
joint and she had ended up crippled for life.

It was then that Ava accidentally knocked her elbow against one of the coffee tables and the lady sitting nearest turned and saw her, letting out a startled scream.

Panicking, Ava jumped to her feet, snatched up her cape, and ran out of the room.

Luckily at that moment the front door was being opened again to admit another of the girls' mothers, and Ava seized her opportunity to escape, dashing past the surprised maid and lady visitor, and racing down the front steps.

'STOP, THIEF!' came an angry cry from behind her – and she quickly realized that the maid was gathering up her skirts to chase after her.

There was nothing for it but to run as fast as she could, with the maid following her as

she sped through the front gate and across
the road to the furniture shop again. As
she reached the door she saw to her horror
that Mrs Potter and the sweep master were
emerging from the side path that led to the
back alley, and when they spotted Ava they
let out loud yells.

Ava slammed the shop door shut behind
her and headed straight for the magic
mirror, without even noticing whether the
old man was at his desk or not. She was just
fastening the cape around her neck when
the master sweep burst in closely followed
by Mrs Potter, but Ava was already staring
hard at her reflection in the mirror, which
had started to glow.

The sweep master was too big to slip
between the heavy pieces of furniture as
deftly as Ava had done, and he swore loudly

as he tried to push
a large leather
armchair out of
his path.

Suddenly a
blinding light filled
the whole shop,
causing Mrs Potter
and the sweep
master to gasp
out loud and
cover their
eyes. And as

Ava closed her own eyes against the glare
she smiled in relief, for she knew that by
the time the light in the shop subsided and
her two pursuers were able to see again she
would be long gone.

★

Seconds later she was back in Marietta's Victorian room, covered in soot and still wearing Florrie's ragged climbing boy's clothes under her cream cape. She briefly wondered what her mother would say if she could see how filthy she was – but there was no time to think of that, because the door suddenly opened and Marietta walked in.

She looked at Ava, first with an expression of utter shock, then one of dismay, until finally her mouth twitched and she began to laugh.

'Whatever happened to *you*?' she asked as Ava removed the cape, now also smudged with soot.

Ava pulled an apologetic face as she replied, 'Quite a lot.'

'Well, I must say I didn't expect you to come back looking like this,' Marietta said.

'That cape is mine, isn't it? But as for the rest . . .' She frowned. 'And *where* is that beautiful tutu?'

'Don't worry, it's quite safe,' Ava explained hurriedly. 'I lent it to a little girl I met there. She's a chimney sweep but she wants to be a ballet dancer, so I persuaded her to audition for a place at Madame Varty's dance school. Madame Varty is the dancer Dad went to interview, you see . . . Anyway Florrie and I swapped clothes so—'

'You gave my beautiful ballet tutu away to a chimney sweep?!' Marietta exclaimed in disbelief. 'Oh, Ava!'

'I told you – I'm going to get it back again,' Ava attempted to reassure her. In fact, she wanted to travel back through the mirror as soon as possible – so Florrie

 128

would still be at the dance school and easy
to find. She already knew from her past
adventures that time passed at the same
rate on both sides of the portals. And she
was desperate by now to know how the
audition had gone, as well as to get the tutu
back.

But Marietta just sighed. 'This is my fault
for encouraging you to go through the
portal by yourself, I suppose,' she admitted.
'Tell me . . . did you meet your dad while
you were there?'

'No,' Ava replied. 'I don't know where
he went. Madame Varty's maid said she
told him he could do his interview later this
afternoon. He hasn't come back here while
I've been gone, has he?'

Marietta shook her head, 'I expect he's
gone off on some guided tour with that

Victorian nanny who seems to have taken such a shine to him.'

Ava scowled, momentarily forgetting everything else. 'He could have taken *me* with him if he has!' she snapped.

'Oh, knowing him, he probably thought the places they were going weren't suitable or something,' Marietta said swiftly, smiling sympathetically. 'He was always worrying about that sort of thing when *I* was young. It's a good job our parents gave me so much freedom before they left or I'd never have seen half the exciting things I did while I was growing up!' Marietta had been sixteen when her parents had disappeared, and Ava could only imagine the arguments there must have been between Marietta and Dad – who had effectively been left in charge of his teenage sister – after that.

Thinking about her grandparents reminded Ava about Marietta's visitor.

'Has your father's friend been yet?' she asked. Although she wanted to travel back through the portal as soon as possible, she was hoping Marietta would come with her this time. She really didn't want to face the master sweep and Mrs Potter again on her own, plus there was something else she wanted to do back in Victorian London – something she was certain would be easier if a grown-up was with her.

'Not yet, I'm afraid,' Marietta said. Seeing the look on Ava's face she added, 'But I'm sure he can't be much longer. Once he's been we can shut the shop and go and do something fun together.'

But Ava shook her head. 'I have to go back through the portal again straight away, but in some different Victorian clothes. This time I need to look like . . . like I'm visiting a posh lady's house for afternoon tea or something.'

Marietta smiled. 'You've another adventure planned already, have you? OK then, I'll go and look out something suitable for you. And in the meantime . . . well . . . you know where my bathroom is.'

'Your *bathroom*?' Ava was momentarily puzzled. 'That's right,' replied her aunt. 'I don't mind you borrowing some more magic

clothes, but before I let you anywhere near
them you're going to need a very good
wash!'

7

In the end Ava wasn't worried about being
recognized by Mrs Potter or the master
sweep when she returned through the
mirror, because in her new clothes she
couldn't have looked more different.

She was clean and tidy again, her blonde
hair pulled back neatly with a pretty
Alice band. While she had been in the
bath Marietta had found her some smart
Victorian day clothes to put on and she now
wore a long-sleeved cream blouse with a
high neckline and a lace collar, tucked into
a gorgeous, very full emerald green silk skirt

that swung when she moved. The skirt came
to just below her knees and was held out
by a surprisingly light,
wire-hoop cage. A
wide frill ran around
the bottom of the
skirt, under which
the additional
white frills of
her pantalettes
peeped out, and
beneath these a
pair of long
white
cotton
drawers
covered her legs
down to her ankles.
On her feet

she wore a pair of dainty-looking, pointy-
toed green leather shoes with little bows
on the front. The clothes were a bit fussier
than Ava was used to but they certainly
made her feel like a very proper Victorian
young lady.

She had brought Florrie's clothes back
through the mirror with her as well, since
Marietta said it was always best to leave
things in the time and place where they
belonged. But as Ava placed the little bundle
of rags out of sight under a chair in the
furniture shop, she hoped with all her heart
that Florrie would never have to wear them
again.

The old man wasn't there this time,
though Ava knew he must be around
somewhere as his shop was clearly still open
to customers. She briefly wondered what

you did if you needed to access the magic mirror after the shop had closed – but she decided it was best not to worry about that at the moment.

She took a deep breath, for there was something important she needed to do. It was so important she had decided to get on with it even before going back to Madame Varty's to look for Florrie, and she felt quite nervous about it.

Ava hadn't said so to Tom and Florrie, but she had made up her mind to go and call on their aunt and uncle herself, to see if she could find out any information about their missing father. Since Florrie had told her that their house was in the next street, and Tom had told her about the lion statue at the front gate, Ava imagined that it shouldn't be too difficult to find. Of course

she didn't know exactly which 'next street'
Florrie had meant, but if necessary Ava
intended to try them all.

A grandfather clock in the shop window
told her that it was mid-afternoon as she
stepped outside and stood for a minute or
two on the pavement, looking to and fro to
see where the nearest neighbouring street
lay. A gleaming horse and carriage suddenly
appeared from around a nearby corner, so
Ava decided that she might as well start
there.

She hurried along the pavement, passing
several dress shops, a children's clothes shop
that had sailor suits and pinafore dresses in
the window, a very posh-looking hat shop
and an upmarket shoe shop. And as she
walked along she couldn't help thinking
how strange it was to be wearing a crinoline

138

skirt. She was certainly glad it wasn't windy or she was afraid she might be tipped off balance and end up displaying her frilly underwear.

The street from where the horse and carriage had emerged turned out to be wide and tree-lined with big detached houses on both sides set back from the road. Some of them had quite grand pillars at the entrances to their drives, but none had a statue of a lion as far as Ava could see. Then, after she had walked quite far up the street and was wondering if she ought to turn back and try a different one, she spotted a house that was smaller than the rest. It had huge yellow pillars marking the entrance to its short, narrow driveway and on top of one of the pillars sat an enormous, rather ugly yellow stone lion. The size of the ornament seemed

completely out of proportion to the size of
the driveway and house, Ava thought. But
it was certainly impossible to miss as you
walked by.

Ava slowly approached the front porch,
starting to worry about what she was going

to say when she got there. The door would probably be opened by a maid who would expect her to have a reason for calling – and to know the names of the people she was calling on! And was it normal for children to pay visits on their own in Victorian times?

She rang the bell before she had time to lose her courage – and the door was soon opened by a freckle-faced young maid who gave her a warm smile as she looked at her questioningly.

Ava smiled back and said, 'I hope I've got the right house – but I . . . I think my friends, Tom and Florrie used to live here . . .'

A very dark expression immediately came over the maid's face as she looked over Ava's shoulder. 'Have you no one accompanying you, miss? No nanny or governess perhaps?'

141

'Er . . . well . . . no . . .' Ava stammered.
'I haven't come far . . .'

'I don't think you ought to have come
here alone, miss,' said the maid, frowning.
'When your parents find out you're gone,
they'll be worried about you, and whoever's
meant to be in charge of you today will get
into trouble.'

Ava tried to look contrite as she said,
'Perhaps, but . . . but . . . I've just moved
back from . . . from away . . . and I wanted
to see if . . . if Tom and Florrie's father had
returned for them yet. They said he'd be
coming back for them one day you see . . .'
She trailed off self-consciously.

The maid kept frowning. 'Haven't you
heard what happened, miss? I don't rightly
know as I should be the one to tell you,
but the fact is the children you speak of ran

away the winter before last.'

'Ran away?' Ava was puzzled.

'That's right, miss. Their father *did* come back for them six months ago – I happened to be the one who answered the door to him. The look on his face was something terrible, it was, when I showed him out after the master had told him the news.'

'Oh, but their father's alive!' Ava exclaimed in relief.

The maid was the one who looked puzzled now. 'Well, yes! Why shouldn't he be? It's *them* that are likely dead by now – the poor foolish little things! That's what the master told their father anyway. They ran away at the start of a very cold winter and no trace could be found of them afterwards. The master and mistress was certain they'd either frozen to death on the streets or that some other harm had befallen them.'

'But . . .' Ava broke off as she tried to make sense of this confusing information. Clearly the children's uncle had lied because he didn't want to admit he had sold his niece and nephew to a chimney sweep. But how was she going to find the children's father now?

'I don't suppose Tom and Florrie's father said where he was staying, did he?' she asked the maid hopefully.

'Well, it's funny you should ask that, miss,' the maid replied. 'On his way out, the poor man asked the master to get in touch with him if he ever heard any news of his children and I saw him hand over a scrap of paper with his address on it. But only this morning I overheard the mistress asking about that scrap of paper and the master told her he'd lost it. It was after a chimney sweep came to the house to speak to her and she got all upset for some reason.'

Ava remembered Tom telling her the sweep had been to visit his aunt and uncle, to offer his services, and had been turned away.

Suddenly a sharp voice sounded from within the house. 'Effie, who are you talking to?'

The maid looked nervous. 'That's the mistress. I'm always getting into trouble for talking too much, miss. Did you want to come in? The mistress *might* speak to you, though I suppose she'd more likely prefer it if you came back later with your mama.'

Ava quickly tried to think what to do. 'Is your master in just now?' she asked. She really didn't want to encounter Tom and Florrie's uncle if she could possibly help it – it would be hard enough just to face their aunt.

'Oh no, miss – the master is out at his club,' Effie replied.

'Then I *would* like to come in, please, Effie,' Ava decided. After all, what did she have to lose?

'Certainly, miss. Who shall I say is calling?'

Ava told the maid her name as she followed her into the hall to wait.

But when Effie returned just a few minutes later she looked upset. 'The mistress was angry with me for talking to you!' she told Ava. 'She says her niece and nephew never mixed with any of the local children when they were here and she doesn't know who you are or why you've come looking for them! She says she wants you to leave the house at once! You'd better

go, miss, for I've never seen her this worked
up!' Effie was already opening the front door
for her.

'Oh, but, Effie, I *have* to find Tom and
Florrie's father!' Ava burst out.

'But why, miss?' asked the maid. 'What
concern can that be of yours?'

And that's when Ava decided to tell Effie
the truth.

'The thing is, Tom and Florrie *aren't*
dead!' she blurted out. 'They didn't run
away either! Their uncle sold them to that
chimney sweep who was here this morning!
That's probably why their aunt keeps
getting upset too – she's obviously feeling
guilty.'

Effie's mouth dropped open and she
looked utterly horrified, as if Ava was
some sort of devil-child who had only just

147

revealed her forked tail and horns. Then her face turned red with indignation as she pointed Ava firmly in the direction of the street. 'You wicked child! How dare you say such things! The mistress was right – I should never have talked to you!'

And before Ava had time to say anything else, Effie had slammed the door shut with an enormous bang behind her.

8

Ava arrived back at Madame Varty's house just as all the girls who had been at the audition were leaving with their mothers. When she saw Ava, the girl called Victoria asked, 'Wherever did *you* disappear to?'

Ava smiled and said that it was a long story but that she had come back to explain everything to Madame Varty.

'Well, I doubt if she'll have time to see you now,' Victoria told her cheerfully. 'There's been a terrible fuss about a girl who came to audition after you left. And you'll never believe it but she had a sparkling tutu

149

just like yours! Very strange and grubby she looked, but Madame let her dance anyway, and you should have seen how wonderful she was! Madame Varty said it was like watching herself at that age, and she got very excited and wanted to know who her mother was, because apparently she was a ballerina too before she died. Anyway, Madame said she would certainly offer her a place in her school, even if she couldn't afford to pay any fees, and she wanted to know where the little girl lived and who took care of her. And then the little girl burst into tears and said she couldn't tell Madame Varty that, and Madame Varty said she must! So the girl ran off down the stairs and, when she came back, who do you think she brought with her but the *chimney sweep*?'

'What happened then?' Ava asked

 150

anxiously, but at that point Victoria's mother took her by the hand and urged her to stop chattering and to come along at once.

'I got a place at Madame Varty's school as well!' Victoria called back to Ava as she accompanied her mother down the drive. 'And what do you think? I was the only other girl who did!'

'That's great!' Ava shouted after her enthusiastically. Victoria would be a nice person for Florrie to have as a fellow pupil, she thought – unlike some of the other girls, who hadn't seemed nearly as friendly.

But before Ava could feel too pleased she had to check what was going to happen now that Madame Varty had discovered who Florrie really was.

Ava stepped into the hall and found herself alone with the sour-faced young

maid who clearly recognized her at once.
'You left your cape here, didn't you, miss?
I'm afraid one of the sweep's boys stole it,
but Madame says she'll buy you another to
replace it if you'll let us know where to send
it. If you'd just like to wait in the drawing
room, miss . . .'

But Ava didn't want to wait in the
drawing room. She could hear raised voices
on the floor above and without waiting for
the maid's approval she ran off up the stairs,
heading for the room where the auditions
had been held.

Inside the room Madame Varty was
engaged in an angry conversation with
the master sweep, who seemed to be
demanding money for something other than
the sweeping of chimneys. Tom was also
there, standing beside Florrie, who was still

dressed in the ballet outfit Ava had lent her.
Mrs Potter was in the room too, glaring and
shouting intermittently at the sweep.

Florrie was the first to notice Ava standing
in the doorway. She said something to Tom
and he immediately turned to look at Ava,
frowning as if he couldn't quite believe what
his sister was whispering to him – that Ava
was the girl she had swapped clothes with in
order to come to the audition.

Ava quickly went over to them, longing
to tell them the good news about their
father.

'Congratulations, Florrie!' she said at
once. 'I hear you did really well in the
audition!'

But before Florrie could respond,
Tom cut in angrily. 'Yes – thanks to *your*
meddling! I can see now that you *was* the

girl sweep I met outside. No wonder you couldn't go up that chimney! You're not a climbing boy! You're a fancy young lady!'

'Well, I wouldn't say I was *that* exactly—' Ava began, but Tom broke in again.

'I don't care *who* you are – you've no right to take away my sister!'

'But I'm not taking her away!' Ava protested. 'I've helped her get a place at Madame Varty's school so she can become a ballet dancer like your mother! I thought you'd be pleased!'

'A ballet dancer like our *mother*!' Tom spat out furiously, raising his voice so that everyone in the room could hear him. 'That's exactly what I *don't* want her to be! I don't want her to end up *falling to her death* like our mother!'

Immediately the whole room fell silent.

'*Falling* to her death?' Florrie repeated, staring at her brother as if he was talking nonsense. 'No she didn't. She got sick with a fever and the angels came and took her to heaven.'

'Pa only told you that cos he thought you were too young to know what really happened to her,' Tom continued hoarsely. 'She were at a rehearsal when a faulty cable snapped while she was being hoisted through the air. She fell on to the stage from a great height and died instantly.' Tom's face crumpled and he started to sob. 'Pa made me promise never to tell you because he thought you'd have nightmares about it. *He* had nightmares about it and so did I! He was

155

watchin' from the wings when it happened
an' he said he couldn't stop thinkin' about
it afterwards an' seein' it over an' over in his
mind. That's why he got so ill and couldn't
look after us any more. That's why he lost
his job and we got kicked out of our house
and he took us to stay with our aunt and
uncle. He said he'd come back for us when
he was better, but I think he never got
better. I think he died of a broken heart.' He
sniffed. 'So you're all I've got left, Florrie,
and I ain't goin' to lose you an' all. You're
not goin' to become a ballet dancer, do you
hear? I won't let you! Pa told me afterwards
of all the other terrible accidents that can
happen to ballerinas – of their dresses
catching fire in the stage gas-lights, or their
feet getting crushed in the trap doors . . .
Believe me, it's safer going up chimneys

than being a dancer – than risking what
happened to our ma!'

All the adults in the room had been
listening in silence, even the sweep master.
Florrie, whose cheeks had become red and
blotchy on her pale little face, started to cry.

Ava stared at Tom in horror, murmuring,
'I'm so sorry, Tom. I didn't know. But
Tom . . . about your father . . .'

Before she could continue, however, the
sweep master started speaking in a cajoling
sort of a voice. 'Now stop yer snivelling,
the pair o' you! Especially you, missy, for it
seems your chimney sweepin' days are over!'
(He had clearly been aware all along that
the child he knew as Fred was a girl, Ava
thought.) The man grinned at Florrie as he
went on, 'It seems you're worth more on
the stage than you are as a sweep, and if this

lady won't pay me what I want for you I'll soon find someone who will! I'm sure there are plenty of theatres looking for talented little girls like you! Now that's a reason for celebratin', ain't it?'

'Oh, you . . . you *odious* man!' Madame Varty burst out angrily. 'Don't worry, you'll get your money, for of course I shan't let this child return to live with you – or let you sell her to anyone else!' She limped over to stand protectively beside Florrie. 'And Tom, you mustn't worry about anything bad happening to your sister while she is at my ballet school. She won't be lent out to any theatres that I do not approve of, or be put in any danger whatsoever. She will have a very good home here with me and I shall ensure that she is properly looked after and educated. But she *must* be allowed to dance!

 158

She is very talented!'

Tom was staring at his sister now – his sooty face streaked with tears. 'Is this what *you* want, Florrie?' he asked her. 'To stay 'ere, I mean?'

Florrie was still crying as she silently nodded at him, before turning to look at Madame Varty. 'But if I does stay here, what will become of Tom?' she asked in a choked voice.

'Why . . . I don't know . . .' the ballet mistress began hesitantly. 'I suppose . . .' She trailed off, clearly not at all sure what to suggest.

Everyone turned to look at Tom then, who was still staring at his sister with a dazed expression in his eyes.

'Oh, don't you worry about me!' he suddenly exclaimed. 'I can take care of

meself!' And before anyone could stop him
he had turned on his heels and run from the
room.

Nobody followed him at first, not even
the sweep master, who was far more
interested in the money he was about to
get in exchange for Florrie than in stopping
Tom from getting away.

'TOM!' Florrie called out, but she made
no attempt to go after him either – maybe
because she knew she wouldn't be fast
enough, or maybe because deep down she
desperately wanted to stay exactly where she
was.

Ava suddenly came to her senses, realizing
that she hadn't yet told Tom about his
father. 'Wait!' she yelled, running out of
the room behind him. 'Wait, Tom! There's
something important I have to tell you!'

 160

She could see him at the bottom of the stairs, heading straight for the door to the servants' corridor. As it banged shut behind him Ava hurried down the stairs, thinking she could catch him by going out the front way and meeting him as he came round the side of the house. She let herself out the front door and raced down the steps and along the side path, imagining that Tom would soon run headlong into her. But there was no sign of him and when she reached the back garden she saw why. Tom had somehow climbed up on to the high back fence and she was just in time to see him jumping down into the alleyway behind it.

'TOM – COME BACK!' she yelled at the top of her lungs.

But it was no good. He was gone and she knew she wouldn't be able to follow him.

I should have told him about his father as
soon as I saw him, she thought tearfully,
feeling furious with herself as she slowly
headed back round to the front of the
house.

Mrs Potter was standing in the doorway
awaiting her return. 'Madame Varty
wishes to speak with you immediately,' she
said, scarcely looking at Ava and obviously
not recognizing her as the same child she
had tried to force up a chimney earlier that
day.

Wearily Ava followed the housekeeper
back up to the audition room, where she
passed the sweep master who was just
leaving. He was grinning and clutching
a large pouch – presumably full of coins.
Madame Varty was alone inside the room

162

and when Ava asked her
about Florrie she was told
that the little girl had been
taken away by one of the
maids to have a bath.

'The child just told
me that the ballet clothes
she is wearing are yours,'
Madame Varty said after
she had dismissed the
housekeeper. 'She says you
lent them to her. Is that
true?'

Ava nodded, adding,
'Please can I have them
back before I go?'

'Of course . . .' Madame Varty paused,
looking searchingly at Ava. 'And my maid
told me earlier that your cape was stolen

by one of the climbing boys . . .'

'Oh, it wasn't really,' Ava told her
quickly. '*I* was the one who ran off with it.
I didn't have anything else to wear when I
lent Florrie my clothes, you see, so I had to
change into hers. And then I remembered
I'd left my cape in your house so I came
back to fetch it before I . . . . well . . . before
I went home and got changed into some
normal clothes again.'

Madame Varty was looking confused.
'I must say I can't quite believe this. You
actually *swapped clothes* with a chimney
sweep?'

'Yes – because I really wanted Florrie to
have the chance to audition!'

'But how could you possibly know that a
common climbing boy . . . or girl even . . .
would be such a good dancer?'

'Because she told me so herself when I spoke to her outside,' Ava said simply.

Madame Varty looked even more perplexed. 'A girl like *you* actually stopped to speak with a sweep's child?'

'Well . . . yes . . .'

'You are a very strange child, to be sure . . . though it's a miracle for Florrie that she met you. She will certainly have a much better life from now on. I have no children of my own and I must admit that I am quite taken with the idea of having a little protégée.' She sighed. 'It is very sad about their mother. It must have happened a few years ago when I was living abroad or I'm sure I would have heard about it. I feel a little sorry that I didn't offer to help the boy too, but I really don't see what role he could have here.'

'There is *one* way you could help him,'
Ava said at once. 'You see, Tom thinks his
father is dead, but *I* know that he's not!'
She quickly told Madame Varty about her
visit to the children's aunt and uncle that
afternoon and what she had discovered
there. 'So if you could help me find their
father . . .'

Madame Varty let out a loud sigh and
went to sit down on the piano stool. 'This is
all too much to take in,' she said. 'First you
bring me this amazingly talented child with
this heartbreaking story about her mother.
And now I find that it doesn't end there . . .
far from it . . . And I still don't know who
you are! You clearly come from a wealthy
home judging by your appearance. But you
seem to be permanently unaccompanied. I
don't understand it. Where do you live and

 166

who are your parents? And why on earth did
you come to audition for me this morning
when you clearly have no interest in ballet
for yourself?'

Ava didn't know what to say, and she felt
tired of lying. But she knew she couldn't
tell Madame Varty the truth. Just as she
was about to start stammering some sort of
reply there was a knock on the door and the
friendly-faced maid entered saying, 'Excuse
me, Madame, but the gentleman who called
earlier is here to see you. I've shown him
into the drawing room.'

'*What* gentleman, Violet?' Madame Varty
asked a little impatiently.

'The one who wants to interview you
about your new school, Madame. You told
him to come back this afternoon.'

Ava only just managed not to gasp out

loud in relief. It was Dad – and she found
that she couldn't wait to see him, even if he
was going to be cross with her for coming
through the portal on her own.

'Oh, yes,' Madame Varty was saying.
'But I am afraid I am rather too tired to be
interviewed today, Violet. For one thing,
I haven't quite finished here yet . . .' She
looked across at Ava. 'If you tell me where
you live, child, I shall send for my carriage
and take you home myself. I wish to speak
personally with your mother or father.'

And suddenly Ava had had enough of
lying and trying to sort everything out on
her own. 'The gentleman who's waiting
downstairs *is* my father, Madame Varty,' she
blurted out.

'I *beg* your pardon?' Madame Varty looked
taken aback. 'Well, if that is true then I

should certainly like to speak with him.
Perhaps *he* can explain why his daughter
roams around completely unsupervised,
attends ballet auditions for no good reason
and swaps her clothes with chimney sweeps!'

Ava gulped. 'Well, the thing is, he doesn't
actually *know* about all that . . .'

Madame Varty looked stern as she replied,
'Really? Well, in that case I imagine it will
prove of great interest to him to find out!'

9

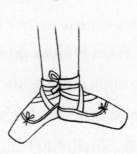

'Ava!' Dad exclaimed in surprise as soon as
he saw her. 'What are *you* doing here?'

Aware that Madame Varty was watching
them closely, Ava replied
carefully, 'I followed you
this morning, but when
I got here
I couldn't
find you, so
I came to see
Madame Varty by
myself.'

'She came to

audition for my ballet school,' Madame
Varty added.

'Audition?' Dad looked puzzled.

'I was wearing a ballet tutu when I first
got here, so it sort of just happened,' Ava
explained.

'What *I* want to know is why your daughter
was allowed to come here unescorted,'
Madame Varty said. 'And to *remain* unescorted
for most of the day, so it seems!'

'Is Marietta not with you?' Dad asked Ava
sharply.

'Marietta is the child's nanny?' Madame
Varty enquired as Ava shook her head.

'Her aunt,' Dad replied grimly. 'The aunt
who was *meant* to be looking after her
today . . .'

At that point Violet knocked on the door
and entered the drawing room holding

171

a small pile of clothes. Ava immediately
recognized the ballet tutu and other items
she had lent to Florrie.

'What did you want me to do with these,
Madame?' the maid asked politely. 'Shall I
wash them or—'

'It's all right – I'll just take them with me
as they are,' Ava broke in quickly.

Violet continued to look at her mistress
questioningly until Madame Varty slowly
nodded her head.

'Wrap them in some brown paper and
bring them back to us as they are,' she told
the girl. She turned to Ava, adding, 'Perhaps
you should explain to your father why we
have them.'

Ava's father was frowning at her. 'Yes,
Ava, please *do* explain.'

So Ava told him all about swapping

clothes with Florrie so that the little girl could win a place at Madame Varty's ballet school. When Ava had finished, Dad looked at the ballet mistress questioningly.

'What the child says is true,' she told him. 'In fact your daughter has done this little girl, Florrie, a great favour. But how she has gone about it . . . well . . . it is a strange way for a girl of her background to behave, I must say. I wonder what your daughter's mother will say when she hears of it. The child *has* a mother I presume?'

'Yes . . .' Ava's father grunted a little cautiously. 'As it happens her mother is away at the moment.'

'Really?' Madame Varty raised one eyebrow, clearly deciding that that explained a lot, before saying smoothly, 'Well, I am not suggesting, of course, that you are having any problems running your household in her absence . . . but I *do* hope your wife will be back soon.'

Ava wanted to laugh at the look on Dad's face, but she just managed to stop herself. Instead she said quickly, 'There's something I really need your help with now you're here, Da— I mean, *Papa*.'

'Oh yes?' He looked at her warily.

'Yes . . . you see, I want to try and find Tom and Florrie's father! Tom is Florrie's brother and he's a chimney sweep too. He ran off just before you got here. It was before I had a chance to tell him that his father is alive, and—'

'Our father is *alive*?' gasped a small voice from the doorway.

Ava turned to see Florrie, her face pink from being scrubbed so vigorously in the bath

and her cropped hair surprisingly fair now
that the remaining soot was gone. She was
standing hand in hand with Violet, dressed
in an adult-sized maroon silk cape, which
covered her from chin to toe. Whatever she
had on underneath it – if anything – was
completely hidden from view.

'I was just about to take her out to buy some new clothes as you requested, Madame—' Violet began, breaking off as Florrie abruptly dropped her hand and took several steps away from her.

Florrie was staring wide-eyed at Ava as she prompted, 'My *father*, miss . . . ?'

Ava looked uncertainly at Madame Varty, who sighed and said, 'Oh dear – I'd rather have waited, but I suppose you had better tell her now.'

Aware that all eyes in the room were upon her, Ava began hesitantly, 'Florrie . . . I . . . I went to your aunt and uncle's house today and I spoke to their maid. She told me your father *did* go back there to look for you. It was six months ago, she says. But your uncle didn't tell him he had sold you to the sweep. He told him that you and

 176

Tom had run away and . . . and that you
had probably died.'

Florrie looked dazed at first. Then she
began muttering, 'I knew he'd come
back for us . . . I knew it . . .' over and
over.

'Yes, but, Florrie, we don't know
where he went after that,' Ava continued
anxiously. 'We have to find him you see,
and let him know that you're still alive.'

'Surely their father would have left a
contact address with their aunt and uncle?'
Ava's dad said.

'Yes, but their uncle lost it,' Ava
explained. 'At least that's what the maid
heard him tell their aunt.'

'Florrie, do *you* have any idea where your
father might be?' Madame Varty asked.

But Florrie just looked at her blankly,

muttering, 'I *told* Tom he'd come back, I
did . . .'

'Florrie, do you know where Tom might
have gone when he ran off this afternoon?'
Ava asked her instead. 'We need to let *him*
know about your father too.'

The little girl turned to face her, seeming
to come out of herself a little. 'Tom might
'ave gone back to the theatre,' she whispered.

'The *theatre*?'

Florrie nodded. 'There's a theatre near
here that we walks past a lot. A few weeks
ago they put a big poster up outside of
a beautiful ballerina. She looks like our
mother did the last time we saw her dance.
We try an' walk by it as slow as we can, but
the master always makes us hurry. Tom got
angry the other day an' said if it weren't for
me, he'd run away and sit across the street

 178

gazin' at that poster all day long.'

'I think I know of which theatre the child speaks,' Madame Varty said.

'So do I,' Dad put in. 'I passed by it myself today. It's the one Marietta told you about, Ava.'

'I suppose someone should go there and look for the boy,' Madame Varty continued. 'I would go myself but I'm afraid I am feeling quite exhausted and my leg is aching badly.'

Ava felt very sorry for the teacher.

'Very well, Ava. You and I will go,' her dad said at once.

'Thanks, Dad,' Ava said gratefully.

'Florrie – I want you to go to the shop with Violet now,' Madame Varty told the little girl gently, pointing her towards the hall where the young maid had tactfully removed herself to wait for further instructions.

'But I want to go and look for Tom,'
Florrie protested.

'I'm sure when Tom hears Ava's news,
he will happily return here to be with you,
Florrie,' Madame Varty told her. 'Ava,
if . . . when . . . you find the boy, please tell
him that he is welcome to stay here with us
while we try to locate his father.'

'Oh, thank you, Madame Varty!' Ava
gushed.

'Come on, Ava, let's go,' Dad said,
standing up. 'And at some point, Madame
Varty, I very much hope you'll allow me
to interview you for the book I'm writing
about reforms in the world of theatre and
dance. I believe your ballet school may
prove to be a leading light in that area.'

Madame Varty inclined her head in

 180

recognition of the compliment. 'When I am
feeling well enough and we have more time,
then I shall certainly grant you an interview.
Now I really must go and rest for a while.'
As she stood up and reached for her cane,
Ava's father offered her his arm. And as they
walked towards the door together she added,
'If you have any problems finding the boy
be sure to ask the theatre manager for his
help. If you mention my name I am sure he
will do all he can to assist you.'

'OK, Madame Varty, we will!' Ava
responded excitedly.

'What a very strange way you do talk,
child,' came the slightly irritated reply – and
Ava could see her father concealing a grin of
amusement as he escorted the still-graceful
ballerina out into the hall.

★

As they made their way to the theatre together, Ava's dad wanted to know everything that had happened to her that day, and he listened without interrupting as she did her best to fill him in as completely as possible.

It was late afternoon by now, but the sun was still shining and there were plenty of people out taking a walk – nannies pushing frilly-bonneted babies in prams, ladies in pretty, light crinoline dresses shielding their faces with parasols, and young men in smart suits and top hats strutting along with their heads held high. There were servants hurrying by too, many of them busy on errands judging by all the packages they were carrying. Children dressed similarly to Ava ran happily along the pavement playing with colourful hoops, while others stood

 182

whipping energetically at brightly coloured
spinning-tops. Inside a small park fenced
off with railings, two little boys in sailor
suits and three little girls in knee-length
crinoline dresses were laughing in a carefree
way as they played marbles together in the

183 ✩ ✩
✩ ✩

sunshine while their nannies chatted in the shade nearby.

Ava wished she felt as comfortable as all the children around her appeared to be, for she was longing to loosen her skirt a little. Also her dainty shoes were rubbing her heels so much that she was sure they were giving her some very *un*dainty blisters.

'Maybe Marietta didn't put enough magic in the leather,' her father commented when she complained to him about the shoes. And not for the first time Ava found herself staring at his perfectly straight face, trying to work out whether he was serious or whether he was joking.

He was certainly being serious when – after she had finished relating all the day's events – he began to scold her severely for coming through the magic portal alone. As

 184

he went on about how foolish she had been she wished she hadn't told him about nearly being forced up a chimney by Mrs Potter or almost getting stranded here after lending Florrie her magic clothes. Just when she thought he had finished telling her off about each of the things that had happened to her, he launched into a list of the even-more-dangerous things that *might* have happened, sounding every bit the stern Victorian father as he concluded angrily, 'I can hardly believe that you disobeyed me and travelled here alone when I expressly forbade it!'

Tearful and defensive, Ava finally snapped, 'Well, I wouldn't have *had* to if you'd taken me with you in the first place instead of going off with that nanny!' She sniffed crossly as she added, 'Marietta says she's

185

taken quite a shine to you!'

Dad stopped scowling and actually laughed at that. 'Don't be silly, Ava. She's interested in me because I'm a travelling person like her, that's all. Today was her day off, so when Madame Varty couldn't see me this morning she offered to show me some places I hadn't been to before. I accepted because it was far too good an opportunity for a historian to miss.'

'Well you could have taken me along too,' Ava pointed out hotly.

Her father shook his head. 'Some of those places weren't at all appropriate for a child to visit, Ava.'

'That's exactly what Marietta *said* you'd say!' Ava exclaimed. 'She says you wouldn't let *her* do anything exciting when *she* was young either! She says it was just as well

 186

your parents gave her so much freedom!'

'Really?' Dad was scowling again now.
'Marietta's childhood memories must
be very different to mine then. What *I*
remember is spending half the time feeling
terrified while our parents dragged me with
them on their so-called adventures – and
the rest of the time being left behind to
look after Marietta! And now it seems my
dear sister can't even manage to return the
favour by looking after *you* properly for a
few hours when I ask her!' He strode along
the pavement in silence after that, with a
face like thunder, but Ava didn't care. She
felt cross too, and she was glad not to have
to speak to him.

Presently they turned a corner into a
much busier street and Ava's father gruffly
pointed out the theatre to her. It was like

187

a giant fairy-tale building, Ava told herself. The facade was very decorative, with pretty scrollwork over the windows and a gleaming green dome protruding from the top of the building. Beautiful winged fairies and woodland creatures were carved into the large mahogany theatre doors, looking for all the world as if they were about to dance off the wooden panels and down the street at any moment.

Several big posters were pasted to the front of the building. They were advertising the show that was currently on – which was indeed a ballet. There was one poster in particular of the principal ballerina dancing en pointe, dressed in a beautiful flowing tutu, wearing a garland of flowers in her hair and an angelic expression on her face.

'That must be the poster Florrie was

 188

Ballet ~ on now

talking about,' Ava whispered as they
inspected it from where they stood on the
opposite side of the road. 'Florrie said Tom
talked about sitting *across* the street to look
at it – which means *this* side of the street,
doesn't it?'

'We'll have to be careful, Ava,' her dad murmured. 'If he *is* here and he sees you before we get the chance to talk to him, he might try and run off again.'

Luckily, at that moment a lady and gentleman moved away from where they had been standing looking in a shop window a little further along the pavement. 'Look, Dad,' Ava said, pointing to what looked like a narrow passageway between that shop and the next.

The two of them walked together as far as the shop – which was directly opposite the ballerina poster – and there Ava's dad took out a shiny coin from his pocket. 'This might allow me to get closer to Tom if he *is* here,' he whispered before taking another step forward and peering into the narrow alley.

 190

Ava guessed at once that *somebody* was there for her father immediately crouched down and offered out the coin, muttering a little awkwardly, 'Here you are, boy!'

Ava held her breath as her dad began to shuffle backwards still holding out the coin, clearly trying to entice whoever was there out on to the pavement.

Ava heard a small cough and a slight scuffle. Then a sooty cap appeared and Ava immediately recognized the tear-streaked little black face peering out from under it.

'*Tom!*' she gasped in relief, rushing over to him. 'Thank goodness!'

And forgetting how dirty he was she flung her arms round him and gave him an enormous hug.

191

10

Ava lost no time in telling Tom about his father, and at first his reaction was the same as Florrie's – he seemed almost too shocked to speak. Then he flopped down on the pavement and began to cry.

Ava thought he would never stop sobbing. In the end she sat down beside him and put her arm round him – ignoring all the strange looks she was getting from passers-by. Her dad didn't seem to care about the passers-by either, for he didn't attempt to stop her.

Eventually Tom wiped his nose and eyes

with his sooty arm and started to ask Ava questions. How had his father looked when the maid had seen him? Had he seemed healthy? Had he given any clue as to where he had been all this time? Had he said where he was staying now or whether he would come back to look for them again?

'Tom, I don't think the maid knew very much at all,' Ava said. 'But don't worry – we're going to do our best to help you find him.'

'Can you remember where you used to live before, Tom?' Ava's father asked now.

Tom told him the name of the street, adding, 'It were in another part o' London – quite far away from 'ere I think, for I remember it took us a long time to get 'ere. We walked for ages and we caught a few rides. And we had to sleep overnight in the street a couple o' times. We didn't have no money by then, what with father's sickness an' all . . .'

'I think that might be the best place to start looking,' Ava's dad said. 'Your father may have moved back there by now or at least got in touch with some of your old friends and neighbours. We'll get ourselves a map of London and find your old street. Oh – and there's one more thing that might help us. Can you tell us if he had a specific trade he might have gone back to? What was his job before your mother died?'

'He were a carpenter, sir,' Tom said. 'He told me that's how he met our mother – he was working on making some stage props – scenery and the like – when he saw her rehearsing. She looked like a butterfly

 194

flitting about the stage, so he said.'

'I see . . . well . . .' Ava's dad looked
thoughtful. 'If that was his job before,
then it's probably worth enquiring about him
in all the theatres closest to where you used
to live.'

'What about the theatres *here*, Dad?' Ava
suggested. 'I'm sure he'd want to stay near
here to look for Tom and Florrie.'

'I don't know, Ava,' her father replied.
'Tom's father may well have begun his
search here – but that was six months ago.
What if he's given up by now? Surely
he'd return to a place that was familiar to
him?'

'But he won't have given up!' Ava
protested. 'I know he won't!'

'This is a much posher area than where
we used to live,' Tom said, frowning. 'I

can't say as I'd know *where* to begin lookin'
for him 'ereabouts.'

Ava immediately pointed to the theatre
directly in front of them. 'What about
there?' she said. 'He's bound to have passed
by it at some point and he might have gone
in to ask if they had any work.'

'Well, it's certainly worth me having a
quick word with the theatre manager now
we're here,' her dad conceded. 'You two
wait out here. I won't be long.'

'You better stand apart from me, miss,'
Tom said as the two children waited
together on the pavement. 'We're gettin'
a lot o' strange looks stood together like
this.'

But Ava shook her head. 'It's obvious
we're together, no matter how far apart
we stand. Look! I'm almost as sooty as you

 196

are now!' She pointed down at her cream blouse, which was badly smudged with soot from where she had embraced him before.

'Don't be daft, miss!' Tom protested indignantly. 'Why, you're as clean as a whistle, you is!'

Ava couldn't help smiling, because it was true that almost anyone, no matter how dirty, would seem as clean as a whistle compared with Tom.

It was only a few minutes later when Ava's father rejoined them.

'Did you find out anything?' Ava asked him eagerly.

Her dad shook his head. 'The manager isn't here today and nobody else seemed willing to talk to me. Apparently he'll be back tomorrow morning so we can speak to him then if we want.'

Tom frowned. 'So what do we do now?'

'We wait – though not here of course.'

And together they headed back towards Madame Varty's.

As soon as they stepped inside Madame Varty's drawing room Florrie shrieked in delight at being reunited with her brother, and Madame Varty had to hold her back from rushing forward to hug him.

'Jus' look at yer!' Tom burst out when he saw his sister. She was wearing a brand-new pale-blue full-skirted dress and pinafore, with a pair of

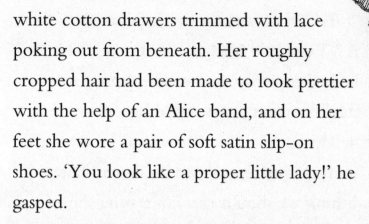

white cotton drawers trimmed with lace
poking out from beneath. Her roughly
cropped hair had been made to look prettier
with the help of an Alice band, and on her
feet she wore a pair of soft satin slip-on
shoes. 'You look like a proper little lady!' he
gasped.

'Are you feeling better, Madame Varty?'
Ava's father asked politely.

'Why yes, I am, thank you,' she replied.
'I shall just have to take care to properly rest
my leg for the remainder of the day, that
is all. I'm afraid too much standing makes
my knee quite swollen.' She sat down stiffly
on the nearest chair, indicating that Ava
and her father should also sit. Tom, she
directed out into the hall, instructing him
to stay there, while Florrie was sent to fetch
Violet.

As they waited for the maid to arrive, Ava's dad told Madame Varty the plan he had come up with so far. 'I propose that Tom and I go back to his old neighbourhood tomorrow and see if we can find out anything about his father. Then I think we should start contacting some theatres in case he's found work again in one of them.'

'We should start with the theatre we just went to, Dad,' Ava reminded him.

Her dad nodded. 'Perhaps you could help us with that, Madame Varty, since you know the manager there?'

Madame Varty inclined her head slowly. 'I am acquainted with him, yes, and I shall be glad to take Ava and Florrie with me to enquire there tomorrow.'

Violet appeared then and Madame Varty

summoned Tom back into the room. 'I want you to go straight in the bath now, Tom,' Madame Varty told him firmly. 'Then we shall see what we can find you to wear. The shop where we bought your sister's clothes normally closes around now, but I think they will be persuaded to stay open a little longer if I send Violet across with another order.'

'I've asked for some tea to be prepared for Florrie in the parlour, Madame. I hope that's all right,' the smiling maid said as she bustled Tom away for his bath.

Madame Varty nodded approvingly, calling after her, 'Thank you, Violet – and please tell Mrs Potter that I shall only require a very light supper myself tonight.' After the maid had gone she commented, 'Violet is *such* a helpful girl.'

'*Unlike* Mrs Potter,' Ava couldn't help adding – and when Madame Varty looked at her questioningly, Ava decided to fill her in. After relating all her unpleasant encounters with the housekeeper that day, she added, 'You'd better watch she isn't cruel to Florrie when you're not there to see it, Madame. And I don't think she likes children in general, so I reckon she might not be very nice to your other ballet pupils either.'

Madame Varty was frowning. 'Do you know, I've had an uncomfortable feeling about that woman ever since I met her. She was with my great-aunt for a long time and she seemed to run the house well enough. There were one or two things about her manner that I thought were odd, but I decided to give her a try since she

obviously knew the house and the local area so well. However, now that you've told me all this, Ava, I think I shall try and find a new housekeeper as soon as I can.'

Ava felt relieved, mainly for Florrie – though it also crossed her mind that perhaps Florrie wouldn't be living with Madame Varty after all if she found her father. 'You'll still give Florrie a place in your school even if she *isn't* living here with you, won't you, Madame Varty?' she asked now.

'Of course,' Madame Varty replied. 'The child can be a day pupil if she wishes. But if she does prefer to reside here with me I will ensure that she sees her family whenever she wants.'

There came a natural pause in the conversation after that and Ava's father

glanced at the clock on the mantelpiece.
'We had better leave you in peace, Madame
Varty,' he said politely. 'What time would
you like us to call on you tomorrow?'

'Shall we say ten o'clock? I will have
the carriage ready and it can drop us off at
the theatre and take you and Tom on to
wherever it is you need to go. The girls and
I can walk home afterwards.'

'Are you sure that won't be too far for
you?' Ava's father asked in concern.

'Oh, no. I like to take a certain amount
of exercise each day,' Madame Varty replied
crisply. 'It stops me from getting too stiff
and becoming even more of a cripple.' She
gave a dismissive little laugh, but a pained
expression had flitted across her face in those
few unguarded seconds, and Ava was quick
to spot it.

'I'm *so* sorry about what happened to you, Madame Varty!' she blurted out passionately. 'I bet you were a *wonderful* ballet dancer before you hurt your knee!'

And Madame Varty's eyes filled with tears as she replied sharply, 'Good gracious, Ava! What an extraordinarily outspoken child you are!'

'I hope Marietta isn't too cross when she sees the state these ballet clothes are in,' Ava said to her dad when they were safely back through the magic portal.

The furniture shop had been closed by the time they got there, but when Ava's dad had rung the bell the old man had let them in anyway. Apparently he lived above the shop and was happy to let them in and out whenever they wished. 'If ever I'm not here, come round the back and there'll always be a key under the flowerpot by the door,' he told them.

Ava frowned now as she put the pile of grubby ballet clothes down on the sofa in Marietta's Victorian room. Only the floral hair wreath, which Madame Varty had also returned, still looked as good as new.

'Don't worry,' her dad reassured her. 'Marietta will probably just send them straight off to the dry-cleaner's.' As Ava looked surprised he added, 'A very *special* dry-cleaner's, you understand.'

Ava guessed that he must mean a dry-cleaning shop run by a travelling family – one that specialized in the cleaning of magic clothes. 'An awful lot of travelling families seem to have shops of one kind or another, don't they?' she commented

thoughtfully as she kicked off her uncomfortable Victorian shoes.

'Every community needs the right shops and businesses to keep it running smoothly,' Dad replied. 'And since our community needs ones that can only be provided by ourselves—'

'I *thought* I heard you in here,' Marietta's breezy voice interrupted him from the doorway.

'Marietta!' Ava and her father both exclaimed at once.

Ava was worried her dad would immediately start interrogating his sister about why she had failed so spectacularly in her childminding duties that day, so she blurted out the first thing that came into her head. 'Marietta, has your father's friend come yet?'

'*Whose* friend?' Dad asked in surprise.

As Ava let out a dismayed gasp, Marietta said quickly, 'Don't worry, Ava. I was about to tell your dad in any case.'

'Tell me *what*?' Dad demanded impatiently.

And Marietta quickly explained to him about the visitor she had been expecting, adding, 'He finally arrived a couple of hours ago. *I* didn't recognize him but he seemed genuine enough. He said his and Dad's families were very close when they were boys. Apparently he hasn't seen or heard from our parents in a very long time, and certainly not since they disappeared twelve years ago. But recently he met some mutual acquaintance of theirs – someone else our father and he both knew when they were young. Anyway, this person gave

 208

him an envelope. He wouldn't say how
he had come by it, just that it was to be
passed on to us and that no one else must
know.'

'An envelope?' Dad sounded tense.

'Here.' Marietta reached into her pocket
and pulled out a small white envelope,
already opened, which had both their
names written on the front in very
distinctive loopy handwriting.

As Ava's dad took it from her he gasped.
'Surely that's Mum's writing?'

'That's what I thought too.'

Dad's hand was trembling slightly as he
pulled out two small cards from inside.
'Invitations to a fancy-dress party!' he
exclaimed in surprise.

'There's one for each of us,' Marietta said.

'Can I see?' Ava asked at once, but

209

her dad
scarcely
seemed
to hear
her as he
studied both
invitations closely.

'It doesn't give the date of the party or say where it is,' he grunted.

'I know, but there was a verbal message too,' Marietta said. 'Apparently we must take these invitations with us whenever we travel anywhere from now on, making sure we check them every time we pass through a portal to see if the date and location have appeared. Then . . . and I quote . . . *one day Otto and Marietta will see their parents again* . . .'

'This man actually said that?'

Marietta nodded. 'So I asked him if he thought the invitations worked in the same way as those theatre tickets . . . that if we take them through the right portal the magic will cause the rest of the details to appear so that we can actually go to this party . . . and he said he presumed so and that he guessed that was where we'd get to see our parents again . . . though it does all seem pretty far-fetched to me!'

'Of course it's far-fetched!' Dad's face was flushed and he sounded very emotional. 'Our parents destroyed the portal they travelled through, and you know as well as I do what that means, Marietta! It means there's no way anyone can ever follow them and no way we can ever see them again – not at some secret fancy-dress party *or* anywhere else!'

Marietta frowned. 'I know all that . . .
of course I do . . . unless . . . well . . .' She
spoke cautiously, lowering her voice as if
she was afraid of being overheard. 'Otto, I
know it's practically unheard of, but what if
they've worked out an *indirect* route to travel
to wherever it is they are?'

Ava's father let out a dismissive snort.
'Indirect routes are notoriously impossible
to map out unless you're some kind of time-
and-space-travelling genius! It would take
forever to make the calculations – and a
much sharper brain than either of theirs to
do it successfully.'

'I agree it would take a long time –
but twelve years *is* a long time,' Marietta
persisted. 'And *I* think our parents were
always a lot cleverer than you gave them
credit for, Otto. I think that's why they

 212

were always exploring places no one else wanted to go. They were trying to discover more about the portal system and how it works – sort of *researching* it if you like.'

But Dad just shook his head as if the whole idea was preposterous.

'So does this mean we *won't* get to see them after all?' Ava asked slowly in a disappointed voice after they had both fallen silent.

'Ava . . . I'm sorry . . .' Dad responded at once, as if only just realizing the effect their conversation might be having on her. 'We really shouldn't be discussing all this in front of you . . .' He glanced quickly at his sister for help.

Marietta backed him up immediately. 'Your dad's right, Ava. The truth is that

213

it's very unlikely we'll ever see our parents again, and it certainly isn't something *you* should get your hopes up about.'

'But *will* you take those invitations with you every time you go through a portal from now on?' Ava persisted, looking from one of them to the other.

Marietta let out a small laugh. '*I* probably will,' she answered. 'You know me – clutching at straws and all that! I really don't expect anything to come of it though.'

'And what about *you*, Dad?' Ava asked him when he didn't reply.

Her dad frowned. 'It would be totally ridiculous even to entertain the idea, Ava,' he told her firmly. But there was something about his response – maybe it was the way he avoided looking at her as he

spoke – which made Ava decide not to
press him further. Instead she gave him a
big hug.

Her father squeezed her back and let
out a barely audible sigh before continuing
awkwardly, 'OK then, Ava . . . well . . .
I suppose it's time I went and got changed
out of these clothes . . .' As he headed
for the dressing room he glanced at
Marietta, who was standing quietly
watching him. 'I don't suppose you
could rustle us up some pasta or something,
could you, Marietta? Then Ava and I
must go home and make sure we both have
an early night. We need to be nice and
fresh for the day that lies ahead of us
tomorrow.'

'Oh – and what sort of day is that?'
Marietta asked him curiously.

215

'It's a long story,' her brother replied. 'But I'm sure Ava will happily tell you all about it over supper, won't you, Ava?'

11

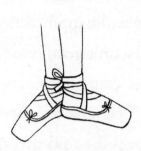

'It seems you were quite right to suggest
that we ask here first, Ava!' Madame Varty
declared the following morning.

Back on the Victorian side of the portal,
Ava had accompanied Madame Varty and
Florrie to the theatre while her father and
Tom (who was looking like a completely
different boy after his bath and change
of clothes) had taken the carriage to the
children's old neighbourhood. The two girls
had been waiting patiently outside while
Madame Varty went in to speak with the
theatre manager, and now she emerged with

a smile on her face, having clearly received some unexpectedly good news.

'Apparently a man *did* offer his services here as a stage carpenter a few weeks back, just after the first advertisements for the ballet went up,' she told them. 'He said that he didn't want money in exchange for his work, but that instead he wanted to be allowed to attend the ballet performance every night. The manager thought that was rather strange, but he offered him the use of a cheap seat up in the gallery. Anyway, this man accepted his offer and he came here and did a full day's work every day while they were getting the set ready. The manager doesn't know where he lives, but he doesn't think it can be that far away because he's been coming here nearly every night without fail to watch the performance. The

 218

man told him his wife was a ballet dancer before she died, and that watching the ballet reminds him of her.'

'Wow!' Ava exclaimed. 'That certainly sounds like it could be your father, doesn't it, Florrie?'

Florrie nodded, looking like she could hardly believe it.

'Oh, but this is wonderful!' Ava cried out, rushing forward to hug Madame Varty, who looked extremely taken aback by her sudden show of affection.

Florrie just stood staring at them, silently smiling. Finally she pointed up at the poster of the principal ballerina. '*She* must be making all this happen from up in heaven,' she murmured shyly. 'Our mother, I mean. An' I've got a funny feelin' about you, Miss Ava, like you're an angel or something sent down to earth to help me and Tom.'

'Well . . .' Ava began, smiling, 'I wouldn't say I was an *angel* exactly, Florrie . . .' And she couldn't help wondering what Florrie would say if she told her where she *really* came from.

If only mobile phones had been invented in Victorian times. Ava could have rung her dad and told him to come straight back. Instead they had to wait until six o'clock that evening before he and Tom finally returned, both looking thoroughly exhausted and downhearted after a fruitless day of searching.

As soon as they heard what the others had discovered, however, they cheered up and Tom immediately began asking excited questions about the man who might hopefully turn out to be his father.

'The manager couldn't remember his
name and I'm afraid he couldn't tell me
anything useful about his appearance either,'
Madame Varty answered apologetically.
'Average height, average build, with an
average sort of face was the description he
gave!'

Tom frowned at that. 'Our father were skin an' bone last time we saw him,' he said. 'He never seemed to eat a thing after we lost our ma. So I don't think you could say he looked *average* exactly . . .'

'Well, if he's better now – and it sounds like he must be if he's well enough to work – then he may have regained most of his weight,' Madame Varty pointed out. 'But you're right, Tom. We can't just *assume* that this man is your father. You and Florrie must meet him for yourselves, and since he apparently hardly ever misses a performance he'll probably be there tonight. This evening's show is sold out apart from two seats in the dress circle – which the manager has presented to me with his compliments – and a few cheap seats up in the gallery, one of which is right next to the seat this man has every night. So I asked for that one as well.'

'You mean . . . ?' Tom was looking at her a little uncertainly.

'I mean that the three of us shall go to the theatre tonight and find out if this man is indeed your father. Florrie and I shall take the two seats in the dress circle and you, Tom, shall have the other.' She glanced at the mantelpiece clock before adding, 'But we shall have to hurry if we are to get there on time.'

Her expression seemed a little strained as she spoke, and perhaps it was that which prompted Dad to say, 'That sounds like an excellent idea, Madame Varty – but are you sure you feel well enough?'

Madame Varty nodded. 'Our seats in the dress circle are very good ones, where I believe I shall be reasonably comfortable,'

223

she told him. 'And I do so love the ballet . . .' She broke off as her eyes filled with tears.

Ava looked at the beautiful ex-ballerina, wondering if it might be difficult for her to watch others dancing on stage now that she could no longer do so herself. But she had a feeling Madame Varty would think it quite inappropriate of her to ask such a question.

'Now . . . I'm afraid we really must go and get ready,' Madame Varty said, rising stiffly to her feet. 'Come along, children. Violet is waiting upstairs to help you get dressed. I just hope the theatre won't be too hot tonight. Sometimes it can be quite unbearable at this time of year.'

'Dad, can *we* go to the theatre tonight as well?' Ava suddenly asked. 'We can use those tickets you left with Marietta!'

Her dad pulled a face. 'Ava, it's already been a very tiring day and we'd need to go back and get changed all over again!'

'*I'm* not tired!' Ava protested. 'And Marietta will help me get changed! Oh, *please*, Dad! If you don't want to take me, then I bet Marietta will!'

'You also have tickets for tonight's performance?' Madame Varty asked Ava's father in surprise.

'I believe my sister has a couple,' he said, letting out a sigh as he looked at Ava's eager expression. 'She'd be more than willing to accompany Ava, I suppose. But, Ava, I'm still not sure that there's enough time.'

'I shall be taking my carriage to the theatre tonight,' Madame Varty informed him. 'I can ask the driver to call in for your sister and Ava on the way if it would help.'

'Oh, no, thank you,' Ava's dad replied swiftly, giving Ava a meaningful look as he added, 'We have our own transport, don't we, Ava?'

And Ava just about managed to keep a straight face as she thought about the magic mirror and agreed that they certainly did.

Ava and Marietta stepped out of the furniture shop that evening to find a small horse-drawn carriage waiting outside with a ruddy-faced driver perched on the top. The shopkeeper had summoned it for them when they'd told him they were going to the theatre, and as Ava climbed aboard first, reaching out to pat the snorting white horse in its harness, she felt as if she was embarking on a wonderful adventure.

Marietta had been only too pleased to

accompany her, and despite the rush to get there on time, she had taken great pains to ensure that they were both dressed perfectly for their night out.

For Ava, Marietta had found a beautiful mauve silk dress with an off-the-shoulder neckline trimmed with a wide lace collar. She had a matching sparkling necklace with a garnet centre, which caught the light whenever she moved. She felt very special. Marietta had also given her some much more comfortable shoes this time – simple flat ones made of gorgeous soft lilac leather. To complete her outfit she wore a pair of lace fingerless gloves and carried a silk drawstring wrist-purse, which had a purple and green beadwork peacock on the front.

Marietta was looking especially radiant in a bronze-coloured floor-length evening

227

gown made of shiny satin, which had bands
of gold lace trim decorating its crinoline
skirt. The bodice had a low neckline and
short lace-edged sleeves and she wore a
gold-coloured triangular shawl around her
shoulders. Her thick copper-coloured hair,
which she had braided at the sides and
pinned into a roll at the back of her neck,
was contained in a decorative hairnet edged
with gold ribbon.

As Ava and her aunt sat side by side in
the carriage, looking out at the street ahead
over the horse's briskly bobbing head,
Marietta pulled off one of her long silk
gloves and reached inside her wrist-purse.
She took out some coins ready to pay the
driver, at the same time retrieving the
theatre tickets and passing them across for
Ava to look at.

228

'See how today's date has magically appeared on them,' Marietta whispered. 'Isn't it amazing?'

'*Everything* about the magic portals is amazing,' Ava whispered back. 'I can still hardly believe I'm really here!'

Marietta smiled at her. 'You'll get used to it. Though I must say some things surprise me even now – like how the magic works on these tickets. They don't even look old and yellow any more, do they? It's just the same with these coins. They were antique-looking on the other side of the portal and now they look like they're fresh from the mint.'

Neither of them spoke about the party invitation Marietta had brought with her, for Ava had already seen Marietta glance at it and confirm that as yet it hadn't undergone a similar transformation.

It didn't take very long for them to arrive at the theatre, where the carriage stopped in the middle of the street for them to disembark. All around them were carriages of different sizes drawing up or pulling away, and there was a great deal of noise and smell from all the horses. Their driver

helped them down, politely accepting
Marietta's coins and wishing them a
pleasant evening before climbing back
on to his seat and driving off again.
Everyone was in their best theatre-
going attire, and the men looked very
smart in their top hats, while the women
rustled their silk skirts and fluttered their
colourful fans. Ava could barely contain her
excitement at it all.

Marietta allowed Ava to lead the way as
they entered the theatre foyer, which was
such a lively bustle of activity that at first
Ava was unable to spot Madame Varty or
the children. Then she saw them standing
close to the door watching all the other
theatregoers arrive. Tom and Florrie must
be trying to spot their father as he came in,
Ava thought. She led Marietta over to join

them, and after the two women had been
formally introduced they stood making
polite conversation while Ava waited with
the impatient siblings.

They stayed where they were until it was
time for the performance to begin, by which
time Tom and Florrie had scanned the
faces of every man who passed by,
but to no avail.

'P'raps he's not
comin' tonight after
all,' Tom said shakily,

and Florrie, who was holding
her brother's hand, looked like she was
about to start crying.

'There's still a chance we may have missed
him in the crowd,' Madame Varty told them
firmly. 'In any case I think we should go
and take our seats now. You *will* be all right

up in the gallery on your own, won't you, Tom?' Madame Varty was looking quite tense herself, Ava thought, though whether that was to do with the lack of appearance of the children's father, or more to do with her own feelings about being inside a theatre as a spectator rather than a dancer, Ava couldn't tell.

'Of course I will,' Tom said, clutching his ticket. 'An' I'll be sittin' right next to him if 'e does turn up. That's all *I* care about!'

'We shall meet you back here at the interval then,' Madame Varty told him, taking Florrie's hand.

'We're in the stalls, aren't we, Marietta?' Ava said.

Her aunt nodded, taking out their tickets to inspect them again as if she half expected the magic to have worn off since she had

last looked. But they were admitted to the
auditorium without question and an usher
immediately directed them to their seats in
the centre of one of the middle rows of the
stalls.

'So what do you think of it all?' Marietta asked her as they looked around.

'It's beautiful,' Ava replied in an awed voice, staring up at the majestic gold domed ceiling. The whole auditorium was extremely ornate, lavishly decorated in rich colours with fancy plasterwork everywhere and an impressive gold arch framing the stage.

It was as she scanned the colourful and noisy audience that Ava noticed many of the ladies fanning themselves furiously – and she soon realized why.

'It's boiling in here!' she whispered to Marietta. 'And it's so stuffy!'

'I know – I think the air conditioning must have broken down,' Marietta joked before pointing to the numerous gas-lamps which lit both the stage and the sides of the

auditorium and adding more seriously, 'All
this gas-lighting eats up a lot of the oxygen,
I'm afraid.'

The mention of the gas-lamps reminded
Ava of some of the things Tom had said
when he told them how his and Florrie's
mother had died – and she wondered if they
were thinking of their mother as they waited
for the curtain to go up. She tipped back
her head to look upward, longing to know
how Tom was getting on up in the gallery.
He would be in one of the highest, furthest-
away seats, but Ava knew that he wouldn't
be nearly so interested in his view of the
stage as in his view of the seat next to him.
Had its occupant turned up yet – and if so,
would it indeed prove to be Tom's father?

Ava sighed, knowing she would have to
wait until the interval to find out. And as

she wiped a bead of sweat from her brow
she wished she wasn't feeling so nervous –
or so hot and sticky – as she waited with
increasing impatience for the ballet to begin.

12

The first act turned out to be a wonderful spectacle, with the ballerinas flitting effortlessly across the stage in their floaty tutus, while the principal dancer, whose picture had so attracted Tom and Florrie by its resemblance to their mother, thrilled the audience with her amazing bounds and leaps.

Ava could see that Marietta was enjoying the performance despite the uncomfortable heat and stuffiness, but Ava couldn't help fidgeting and wishing for it to be over. Neither Marietta nor Ava had a fan, and

Ava found herself thinking longingly of the little hand-held battery-operated one that her mother always carried around in her bag during the summer.

At last the curtain dropped on the first act and they could leave their seats, though that turned out to be a long process as they had to wait for everyone else to move out first. When they finally reached the aisle, a lady just ahead of them suddenly fainted, and there was a huge kerfuffle while she was given smelling salts to revive her. Ava thought it was surprising that more people weren't fainting in the airless atmosphere, and she noticed quite a few heading for the open theatre doors as soon as they reached the foyer.

'Look!' Ava exclaimed excitedly to Marietta. For over by the doors, close to where they had been standing before, she could see Tom and Florrie being embraced by a slim young dark-haired man who had tears streaming down his face. Madame Varty was standing a little further away, smiling.

'Maybe we should wait for a minute before—' Marietta began, but Ava had

already left her side and
rushed over to her friends.

'Tom! Florrie!' she
called out in delight.
'You found your father!'

As Ava stood beaming
at the little huddle
Marietta went to join
Madame Varty, and
the two women spoke
together in quiet voices
for a minute or two.
Then Madame Varty announced, 'As my
carriage is waiting outside I think we should
all leave now rather than waiting until the
end of the performance.'

She led them to her carriage, which was
much larger than the one in which Ava and
her aunt had travelled to the theatre, and

241

was drawn by not one but a pair of beautiful grey horses. It had two double seats facing each other, and Marietta and Madame Varty sat together on the forward-facing seat while Tom and Florrie's father sat (looking dazed) on the reverse-facing seat with the three children.

On the journey back Tom told how he had been too upset by his father's lack of appearance to concentrate on the ballet, so had slipped out just before the end of the first act. Down in the foyer he had immediately spotted a familiar-looking man who was standing very still, gazing at the poster of the beautiful ballerina.

'He got there late so he was waitin' to take 'is seat after the interval, wasn't you, Pa?' Tom said, at which his father nodded silently in reply.

'Did you recognize each other straight away?' Ava wanted to know.

Tom looked expectantly at his father, who swallowed and spoke shyly for the first time. 'Not immediately,' he admitted hoarsely as he twisted his head to look at Tom with a very soft expression in his eyes. 'Tommy's changed a lot, I must say.'

'But I recognized 'im all right,' Tom added quickly. 'An' it didn't take you long to see that it was me under all these posh clothes, did it, Pa?'

'Your clothes are not *that* posh, Tom!' Madame Varty half smiled, half reprimanded.

'They're not?!' Tom exclaimed, and he had such a look of shocked disbelief on his face that everyone in the carriage, including Madame Varty, started to laugh.

★

Once they were all sitting comfortably in Madame Varty's drawing room, sipping cups of tea and eating the dainty triangular sandwiches that Violet had prepared for them, Tom's father explained where he had been for the last two years. He flushed with shame as he told how he had gone to the dreaded workhouse initially, where he had been forced to work hard despite being sick, and had suffered terribly from illness and malnutrition during the first few months. But miraculously his health had slowly improved until he had grown strong enough to leave and look for a job outside. Believing his children to be better off with their aunt and uncle, and feeling too disgraced by his recent experience at the workhouse to dare contact them, he had travelled out of London and found work as a carpenter repairing a church that had been partly destroyed in a fire. The vicar had been a kind man who had counselled him a great deal and helped him come to terms a little with his wife's death. He had stayed there until the job was finished, receiving plenty of food, shelter at night in a nearby barn, and a small amount of money in exchange for his labour. When he had finally returned to London, feeling able at last to take care of his children, he had heard the terrible news that they had run away. He had been devastated, blaming himself for not returning for them earlier – and he had been searching for them ever since.

'We never did run away,' Tom told him now. 'We've been workin' for a chimney sweep all this time.' And he related the whole story to his father – who sat and listened with a stunned expression on his face.

'Your uncle *sold* you to this sweep?' he kept repeating when Tom had finished. 'Why . . . I'll . . . I'll . . .' His cheeks were reddening in anger now.

'The children's uncle – is he your brother?' Madame Varty asked him quickly.

Tom's father shook his head. 'My wife and his were sisters,' he explained. 'My wife was judged to have married beneath her and she was more or less cut off by her family afterwards. But I thought maybe my wife's sister and her husband might take a shine to the children after she died, specially as they had none of their own. But obviously I was wrong.'

'Well, *I* think you should stay well away from them from now on,' Madame Varty told him briskly. 'It certainly won't help the children if you end up getting into a fight with their uncle, possibly being arrested. I think it best if you leave it to me to call on their aunt to make sure she knows that others are aware of what she and her husband did. We shall have to think very carefully about what else we do with the information – if anything.' She glanced briefly at Florrie, who was leaning tiredly against Tom, absent-mindedly tugging at the lace hem of her dress. 'Now . . . where is it that you reside at present?' she asked their father.

'I've just a small room in a lodging house at the moment, but I've got work now and I know where I can get more after this. The children will have enough to eat and a warm place to sleep at night, so you don't have to worry about them no more,' he assured her at once.

'Of course not,' Madame Varty said tactfully. 'But what I haven't told you is that I have already offered Florrie a place in my new ballet school – a totally free place you understand – for I believe she has the makings of a very talented dancer.'

'A dancer, eh?' Florrie's father swallowed as he added, 'Like her ma . . .'

Everyone in the room fell silent, for it was obvious that he hadn't completely got over his wife's death – or the way it had happened.

Madame Varty paused respectfully for a little while longer before continuing more gently, 'What happened to your

248

wife was a terrible tragedy, but I want you
to know that I shall be taking the utmost
care to ensure the safety of all my pupils.
Of course we must discuss this further and
you may ask me any questions you wish.
But I should also say that I have offered
Florrie free board here in my house and –
if you are in agreement of course – I would
be delighted to have her live with me.
Naturally you and Tom may see her as
often as you wish.'

'Well . . .' Florrie's father was clearly
feeling more than a little overwhelmed by
the turn of events. 'I'll . . . I'll . . . have
to think on it,' he stammered. 'But . . .
well . . . what do *you* say, Florrie? Would
you like to live here with this lady and learn
to dance like your ma, while Tom learns to
be a carpenter like me?'

'Oh yes, Pa, for I want to be a ballet dancer more than anything!' Florrie burst out at once. 'An' it's what our ma wanted me to be too!'

'I know she did, Florrie, and I know it ain't right to stop you if you're as good as she was . . .'

'I think it is highly likely that she *is*,' Madame Varty put in, smiling at Florrie, who gave her an even bigger smile back.

'An' if that's how it is, then I'd rather you went to a good school where you'd be safe . . .' Florrie's father continued, but at that point his voice cracked and they saw that he was blinking back tears. 'But for tonight all I want is for the three of us to be together,' he said. 'Like I said, my lodgings aren't far from here and we can come and see you again tomorrow,

 250

Madame Varty, to talk about the rest.'

'Well, of course,' Madame Varty agreed at once.

Marietta stood up too then, saying, 'Come on, Ava. It's time we were getting home as well.'

'Would you like me to summon the carriage for you?' Madame Varty asked.

'Oh, no, thank you, it's only a short walk from here,' Marietta replied quickly. 'But there is just one more thing . . . My brother asked me to check if it would be convenient for him to come and interview you for his book tomorrow morning.'

'Of course,' Madame Varty said. 'He may call on me at ten o'clock.'

'Thank you – and you don't mind if Ava comes with him, do you? I'm rather busy tomorrow and won't be able to look after her myself. And as I think you know, her mother is away at the moment . . .'

Madame Varty frowned. 'Of course Ava may accompany him, but I must say I find it most strange that the child has no nanny or governess to take care of her.'

'It *is* a little strange, isn't it?' Marietta said carefully. She looked at Ava, adding, 'After all, it's certainly not that your father has anything *against* being out and about in the company of a nanny – is it, Ava?' And she gave her niece a little wink.

Ava only just managed not to giggle as she called out, 'See you tomorrow, Madame Varty!' and quickly followed Marietta out into the hall.

Tom, Florrie and their father left the house along with them, and at the bottom of the drive they all paused to say goodbye.

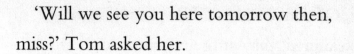

'Will we see you here tomorrow then, miss?' Tom asked her.

'Oh, yes,' Ava said. '*If* Da— I mean Papa lets me come with him, that is.'

'He'll let you. Don't worry about that,' Marietta reassured her. 'He's got some quite exciting plans for you and him tomorrow, I believe.'

'Really? What plans?' Ava asked in surprise.

'Oh, I think I'd better let him tell you about that!' Marietta said, smiling.

'Thank you so much for everything you've done for my children, miss,' said Tom and Florrie's father, looking gratefully at Ava.

'Yes,' Tom said at once. 'I'd give you a hug, miss, only I don't think it would be proper.'

'Of course it would be proper!' Ava exclaimed, throwing her arms round him and squeezing him tightly. She hugged Florrie too, who seemed to want to say something else before they parted.

'I meant it when I said I thought you was an angel, miss,' she whispered, flushing.

Ava laughed as she whispered back, 'I'm certainly not an angel, Florrie, but . . . well . . . I'm not exactly a *normal* person either!'

When they arrived back through the portal and had changed into their normal clothes, they went to find Ava's dad. He was sitting at the kitchen table, making notes for his new book.

'Well? How did it go?' he asked them.

Ava immediately filled him in on

everything that had happened. 'Isn't it wonderful that Tom and Florrie have found their father again?' she finished.

'It certainly is,' her dad agreed, smiling at her. 'And that's largely down to you, Ava. I know I'm always saying that we shouldn't interfere too much in the lives of the people we meet on the other side of the portals, but actually in this case I'm very glad that you did.'

'Madame Varty says it's fine for you to go back there tomorrow morning to interview her, Otto,' Marietta told him.

'Good,' Dad said. 'Listen, Ava . . . tomorrow you can come with me to Madame Varty's house and once I'm finished there I'll take you on a proper tour of Victorian London – just the two of us. Would you like that?'

'Oh, yes, please!' Ava burst out excitedly.

'We'll have a look at a map together and we can plan out exactly where we want to go.' He paused. 'But, Ava, after tomorrow I'm afraid I shall have to spend quite a bit more time working.' He turned to Marietta. 'I'm hoping I can rely on you to entertain Ava for the next few days – *without* letting her go through any more portals unaccompanied, that is.'

Quick as a flash, Ava asked, 'Does that mean I can go through some more portals as long as Marietta comes with me?'

'See, Otto!' Marietta exclaimed delightedly. 'Like it or not, Ava has the same adventurous spirit as everyone else in our family!'

Ava's dad let out a resigned sort of sigh. 'I suppose if Marietta goes with you, then I can't object too much, Ava,' he said.

'Just as long as she doesn't take you anywhere I wouldn't be happy to take you myself.'

'Oh, I wouldn't dream of it, Otto!' Marietta assured him, giving Ava a conspiratorial wink. And she went on to describe a number of particularly exciting fantasy lands, which she was sure Ava would love, and which were remarkably safe as well. 'Apart from the pirates, of course,' she added with a mischievous grin.

'*Pirates?*' Ava's dad queried with a frown.

'Yes, but you don't have to worry, Otto,' Marietta replied cheerfully. 'Ava and I can both swim, so I'm sure we'll be fine, even if they do make us walk the plank!'

'Marietta, this isn't funny . . .' her brother grunted.

257

But Marietta
clearly thought
that it was,
and as she
started to
giggle her
laughter was so
infectious that
Ava found it impossible not to join in.

**There are hundreds of beautiful dresses in every
colour of the rainbow — sewn with magic thread.
Take a look, try one on — and wait for the magic
to whisk you away on an amazing adventure!**

Ava is looking for her cat when she finds Marietta's
mysterious shop. She tries on a perfectly fitting gold and
emerald princess dress and whizzes through a secret
mirror — to fairytale land! Will she get there in time
to be a bridesmaid at Cinderella's wedding?

There's a secret world at the bottom of the sea!

Rani came to Tingle Reef when she was a baby mermaid –
she was found fast asleep in a seashell, and nobody knows
where she came from.

Now strange things keep happening to her – almost as if
by magic. What's going on? Rani's pet sea horse, Roscoe,
Octavius the octopus and a scary sea-witch help her find
out . . .

Ellie is delighted when she goes to visit her aunt and meets Myfanwy and Bronwen, the valley fairies.

And when the fairies invite Ellie to a meeting at the tiny toy museum in the village, she learns one of the biggest fairy secrets of all. With a little bit of fairy dust, toys can come to life!

But the museum is about to close, and with it the enchanted entrance to Fairyland. Can Ellie come up with a plan to save them all before it's too late?

'A-A-A-TISHOO!' Cosmo burst out, sending a huge shower of magic sneeze into the cauldron.

Cosmo has always wanted to be a witch-cat, just like his father, so when he passes the special test he's really excited. He can't wait to use his magic sneeze to help Sybil the witch mix her spells.

Sybil is very scary, with her green belly button and toenails, and no one trusts her. So when she starts brewing a secret spell recipe – and advertising for kittens – Cosmo and his friend Scarlett begin to worry. Could Sybil be cooking up a truly terrifying spell? And could the extra-special ingredient be KITTENS?

A purr-fectly funny and spooky story starring one brave kitten who finds himself in a cauldron-full of trouble.

Website Discount Offer

Get 3 for 2 on any of the Fairy or Cosmo
series at www.panmacmillan.com

£1 postage and packaging costs to UK addresses, £2 for overseas

To buy the books with this special discount:

1. visit our website, www.panmacmillan.com

2. search by author or book title

3. add to your shopping basket

Closing date is 31 October 2011.

Full terms and conditions can be found at www.panmacmillan.com

Registration is required to purchase books from the website.

The offer is subject to availability of stock and applies to paperback editions only.